Riot School

Riot School

Robert Rayner

James Lorimer & Company Ltd., Publishers
Toronto

James Lorimer & Company Ltd., Publishers acknowledges the support of the Ontario Arts Council (OAC), an agency of the Government of Ontario, which in 2015-16 funded 1,676 individual artists and 1,125 organizations in 209 communities across Ontario for a total of $50.5 million. We acknowledge the support of the Canada Council for the Arts, which last year invested $153 million to bring the arts to Canadians throughout the country. This project has been made possible in part by the Government of Canada and with the support of the Ontario Media Development Corporation.

Cover design: Tyler Cleroux
Cover image: Shutterstock

978-1-4594-1170-8
eBook also available 978-1-4594-1168-5

Cataloguing data available from Library and Archives Canada.

Published by:
James Lorimer & Company Ltd.,
Publishers
117 Peter Street, Suite 304
Toronto, ON, Canada
M5V 0M3
www.lorimer.ca

Distributed by:
Lerner Publishing Services
1251 Washington Ave N
Minneapolis, MN, USA
55401
www.lernerbooks.com

Printed and bound in Canada.
Manufactured by Friesens Corporation in Altona, Manitoba, Canada in December 2016.
Job #228982

*Thanks to Darlene Thompson,
Claire Thompson, and Nadia Habib for
help and advice.*

Riot School *is for Duncan.*

Chapter 1

Protest

It's more carnival procession than demonstration. A group of high school kids straggle down Atlantic Avenue, taking up most of the road. Girls in purple and yellow cheerleader outfits. A Lion, a Scarecrow, a Tin Man, and a pigtailed Dorothy — the drama class — ready, like the cheerleaders, for after-school practice. Basketball players in purple and yellow uniforms throw needlessly hard chest passes and leap to shoot imaginary baskets. A group of girls, taking advantage of the end-of-year relaxation of the school dress code, strut with stomachs exposed between white denim short shorts and lacy, see-through tank tops.

They wave as cars weave slowly through the group. Some drivers smile and wave back. Others scowl and blow their horns.

Bilan Mahamoud, in a green hijab and short red jacket over a long, dark green dress, marches at the head of the students. Arn Saunders, in black jeans with a hoodie covering his almost shaved black hair and part of his dark face, is beside her. Barlow Fist has his cap pulled so low it rests on his sunglasses, and shoulders hunched in an army surplus jacket over a tee shirt with *Like I Care?* on the front. He saunters among the cheerleaders, who cartwheel and pirouette around him. Grant Mograno swaggers with his basketball teammates. At the rear — part of the group but not part of it — Lettie Snow drifts with her eyes on the ground.

Then, from a car creeping through the crowd, "Why don't you go back to where you came from?"

It doesn't often happen in the little seaside town of Savage Harbour, but Arn and Bilan, at the head of the procession, are always ready for it. Arn steps directly in front of the car, forcing it to stop. The driver — male, middle-aged, red-faced, balding — climbs out. He marches close to Arn and says, "Move your black arse out of the way of my car."

A police cruiser appears, moving slowly towards the students.

Barlow moves to the front of the group and murmurs to Arn, "Best let it go."

The driver grins, pointing his finger at Arn. "You heard your friend, *boy*. Back off."

Barlow steps between Arn and the driver. He puts his hand on the driver's chest and says, "No. You back off."

The driver scoffs, "Or what?"

Without taking his eyes from the driver, Barlow slowly takes off his sunglasses. He holds them out and Bilan takes them. Barlow says, "Or I'll beat the crap out of you, right here in front of everybody."

The driver hesitates, then scurries back to his car, making monkey noises as he goes. As the man pulls away, Barlow takes his sunglasses from Bilan, who murmurs, "Thank you."

Arn snarls at Barlow, "Why don't you keep out of my way? I don't need you to fight my battles."

"I know," says Barlow. "But the thing is — I can punch out dickheads like that and nothing will happen to me. You do it and you're in shit."

Bilan says, "He is right, Arn." She takes his arm and pulls him away. But Arn still scowls back at Barlow.

The police car has stopped a few metres up the street with lights flashing. Sergeant Tony Hansen notes the registration of the car that's pulling away as he approaches the students. A few minutes earlier he was reading the *Atlantic Daily News* with his feet on his desk and a cup of coffee in his hand. Then the secretary called from the front desk: "Got a call from St. Isaac's School about kids walking out. The principal wants the police to stop them." Sgt. Hansen was half inclined to ignore the call. It was a warm June morning near the end of term. The kids always walked out at least one day this time of year, usually to go to the beach. It was like a tradition. He'd done it himself. But nothing else was on, so he decided to take a look. He headed down to Atlantic Avenue, which ran alongside Seaside Park, where the old school sat like a stately home.

He knows some of the students by name, all of them by sight. He's had a few run-ins with a couple of them, namely Arn and Barlow. He has his men keep an eye on the strange girl at the back, the one he sees on the street at all hours of the day and night. And then there's the immigrant girl at the front of the group. He's uneasily aware it may not be correct to think of her like that, but he doesn't know her name.

He leads the students to the sidewalk and asks, "What's going on, guys? What are you doing out of school?"

The girl, who seems to be the leader, has her hands on her hips. A pretty kid, with skin the colour of amber, she barely comes to his chin. But she stares at him like a challenge. He thinks that if her eyes could shoot fire he'd be burned to a crisp.

"We are demonstrating," she says. "And you cannot stop us." Her voice is taut, her diction perfect.

"Whoa," says Sgt. Hansen. "I'm not trying to, not unless you block traffic or cause a major disturbance, Miss . . . er . . ."

"Mahamoud. *Ms.* Mahamoud."

"Sorry. Ms. Mahamoud. Just, it would have been helpful if you'd let us know you were planning to demonstrate. Maybe I could have helped with traffic control."

"We do not need help. Thank you."

"So who's in your group?"

"The grade eleven class. The principal said we were not allowed to protest because children — children! — did not have the right to question decisions made by the authorities."

"That'd be the decision about the school?"

"Which means the decision concerning our future."

"Where are you marching to?"

"The town hall, where the District Education Council is meeting."

"How about I follow you, keep the traffic back?"

"Then you will harass us when we get to the town hall."

Sgt. Hansen sighs. "I'll stay out of your way, unless something happens that needs my attention."

Chapter 2

We Will Be Heard

With Bilan at their head, the students march
the three blocks to the town hall, a narrow,
three storey, brick building. Charlie Higgs,
the door guard, with rounded shoulders and
a shock of white hair, sees them approaching.
He stands in the doorway with his arms held
wide and says firmly, "Sorry, young ladies and
gentlemen. You can't come in."

Bilan says, "But we want to address the
Education Council."

"The meeting's private. Sorry, dear. Best I can do is take a message."

"Please ask the council if we can talk to them about St. Isaac's School."

Charlie Higgs returns a few minutes later, shaking his head. "I spoke to the superintendent of schools, Mr. Kitchener. He says students are not allowed to attend meetings of the council. He says the principal of St. Isaac's has informed him you have left the school unlawfully and you are to return right away."

Bilan purses her lips. "What room are they in?"

Charlie Higgs nods at the ground floor window beside him.

She turns to face the window and starts chanting loudly, "We have a voice and we will be heard."

She looks around at the students, cupping her ear. They repeat after her, uncertainly at first, then louder as Bilan goes on. "We have a voice and we will be heard."

Barlow uses a garbage can as a drum to beat out the rhythm. The students stamp their feet with him. Their voices grow louder. Charlie Higgs, watching from the doorway, moves his shoulders with the beat. Sgt. Hansen, who has parked across the road and is leaning on his car, smiles.

A rock sails from the group. It shatters the window of the room right above the room where the meeting is being held.

The chanting and stamping and drumming falter and stop. Charlie Higgs rushes into the building.

Sgt. Hansen mutters, "Stupid." He saw who threw the rock. He starts across the road, but stops when Charlie Higgs comes out again. He is followed by a tall, sharp-featured woman wearing a pale grey business suit. She looks at the students over her glasses and announces, "I am the mayor, Ms. Sally Burr. I was in my office and heard breaking glass."

Bilan steps forward. "We are sorry. Someone in our group threw a rock. We take full responsibility and we will take a collection to pay for the damage."

Sgt. Hansen thinks, *Well done, Ms. Mahamoud.*

The mayor says, "But what are you doing here?"

"We are demonstrating. We want to address the Education Council but they refuse to let us in."

Ms. Burr smiles. "It's good to see young people taking an interest in political affairs. But breaking windows does your cause no good."

Bilan repeats, "We are sorry."

The mayor goes on, "If you're willing to pay for the damage and promise not to let any future demonstrations get out of hand, then the Town will overlook the misdemeanour."

"We will pay in full, and we will clean up right now if you like."

Ms. Burr smiles again. "Not necessary."

As the students move away, a tall, heavily built man in a dark blue suit comes to the door. He has thinning grey hair and thick eyelashes that stick out like fins. Sgt. Hansen recognizes the superintendent of schools straight away. He's surprised it's taken Stafford Kitchener this long to make an appearance. At meetings of the school and community liaison committee, the superintendent always presses the police to take a more active role in disciplining the youth of the town. At the last meeting he proposed an eight o'clock curfew for everyone under the age of sixteen.

Stafford Kitchener says, "What happened?"

Ms. Burr says, "Just a broken window. Nothing serious."

"Did the children do it?"

"Yes. But they've apologised and agreed to pay for the damage."

Stafford Kitchener turns to Sgt. Hansen. "I want them disciplined."

"What for?"

"Vandalism. Breaking the window."

"Ms. Burr has already forgiven that."

"For truancy, then."

"That would be the school's job, not ours."

The superintendent glares at him. Then he turns and stalks back into the town hall, brushing past the mayor and Charlie Higgs.

Sgt. Hansen hurries after the students, who are straggling across the road. He walks beside Bilan Mahamoud. "You handled that well. I know who threw the rock. I may have a quiet word with him later on, but no more than that."

"Thank you."

"Is that the end of your protest?"

She stops and looks up at him. He thinks, *What amazing eyes.* Huge and almond-coloured. He doesn't think he could look away if he wanted to.

"Oh no," she says quietly. "It is just the beginning."

Chapter 3

Barlow

Two months later, two weeks before the new
term begins, Barlow Fist is on his way through
Seaside Park. He's going to check out the
best way to break into St. Isaac's School. He
browses through the Savage Harbour tourist
brochure as he walks, hoping it makes him
look innocent. He grabbed it a few seconds ago
from Grant Mograno, who's standing at the
main gate. Dressed in a blazer and white shirt
and tie, Grant hands them to tourists visiting

the thirty-five acre park that surrounds the historic school.

Barlow smiles when he thinks about Grant saying, "You can't have that."

Barlow, turning and walking backwards, said, "So what are you going to do about it?"

He knows Grant won't come after him. He can't get into trouble while he's doing his summer job. It is no surprise Grant snagged himself one of the town's summer positions, since his father is on the council. Grant is welcome to it. Barlow wouldn't get himself up like that even if they paid him.

He sits on a bench at the edge of the trees, waiting for the chance to stroll over to the school. He stretches out his legs. Hands behind his head, he looks around casually, just another tourist enjoying the late August sun. No one nearby. Grant was watching him a moment ago, like Barlow was somehow suspicious. But now he's busy with a group of tourists.

Barlow strolls through the wooded area of

the park. He comes to the edge of the trees and checks all around again. Then he walks smartly across The Meadows, the expanse of grass that surrounds the old school. He looks around again. Still no one near, no one looking. He sidles around to the back of the school and stops at the first classroom window, his old homeroom. He cups his hands to each side of his face to keep reflections off the glass as he peers in and studies the window latch. It's still broken, like it has been for years. No need to even break the glass, just ease it sideways and climb through.

He looks around the room. It's just as it was at the end of term. He runs the numbers. Four computers, four monitors, $1,000 right there. Another four in each classroom, six classrooms, that'll be $6,000. A dozen in the library, two in the office. Another $3,500. He could get at least $20 for each desk but he's not sure they're worth the bother. He moves on to the next window. It looks into the gym.

Basketballs, soccer balls, volleyballs, at least a hundred. They would be a bargain at $5 apiece. Cross-country skis, maybe a couple dozen of them, $75 a set. That's around $10,000 altogether and there is probably more stuff he can't see. He grins. He'll be able to retire for a while, even cutting in Dean, his twenty-one-year-old brother.

So, early hours of the morning, Barlow and Dean will drive his brother's van in on the service road that comes off Shore Road beside the park, lights off. They'll park on the rough grass behind the school. In through Barlow's old homeroom window, open the double gym doors to take the stuff out. No one will hear and he knows the school has no alarm, never has, what with the people of Savage Harbour being such friendly, trusting folk. They're famous for it, more fool them. With luck, no one will even know about the break-in for weeks.

He moves on to the next classroom and

looks in to see what's worth taking. He jerks back, thinking he sees movement in the hallway on the other side of the classroom. He peers in again, cautiously. No sign of movement now. He must be imagining things. Still, he feels spooked. But he knows enough.

He just has to choose the best night to break in. And he already knows when that will be.

Chapter 4

Lettie

Lettie wakes up on the staff room floor. She knows it's late, but it doesn't matter. It's August, so there's no need to worry about anyone walking in on her. She had camped in St. Isaac's in the winter term when she couldn't find anywhere else and was afraid of freezing if she slept on the street. Then, she liked to be up and dressed and hidden in the washrooms by six o'clock, when the custodian came on duty. She hid there until the kids started arriving at eight. Or she sneaked out and got breakfast at McDonald's and returned to school as if she was coming from home — a home she doesn't have, not since her parents split.

She falls into a half-sleeping daydream as she remembers her parents leaving. Her father hugged her and said, "I'll only be out west a few months, until jobs start opening up here." Her mother and her new man decided they'd move to Newfoundland, where he could work for his brother in the oil business. Lettie, not wanting to leave St. Isaac's and Savage Harbour, told her father she was staying with her mother. Then she told her mother she was joining her father. When her mother and her man dropped her off at Laneyville Airport as they set off, Lettie cashed in the plane ticket they'd bought her and caught the bus back to Savage Harbour. She knew she'd get away with it unless her parents talked. And how would they do that when Lettie had been the go-between for the last two years?

Now she squats wherever she can find somewhere for the night. Sometimes it's the Savage Harbour Museum, where she hides in a coat closet until the staff locks up, then leaves early in the morning before the cleaners arrive. Sometimes it's the summer cottage that has been for sale forever, getting in through a basement window with a missing latch. She sleeps on the beach on fine nights. She doesn't know how she'll manage when term starts in September. But she can probably still sleep in the old school at least some nights, at least for a while, although it will be different.

But then, it will be different for all the kids.

She decides to take a shower. She hates the change rooms when they're crowded and noisy, but she likes them now that they're as silent and empty as the rest of the school. She sets off down the hallway, glancing in the empty classrooms. Something stops her. Someone's peering through one of the windows in her old homeroom, hands cupped around the eyes, nose pressed against the glass. Tourists are usually content to look at just the front of the school. She draws back, waits a few seconds, then peeks in the room cautiously. There's no one at the window now. It must have been a tourist, or little kids fooling around.

Lettie takes a long shower and dresses in one of her two outfits, both jeans and a sweatshirt. She has one set to wear while the other dries. She glimpses herself in the mirror. She looks at the dirty blonde hair hanging around her shoulders, her short, scrawny build. Her old-fashioned glasses with the thick black rims would be cool retro on other girls, but on her are just sad. She looks away quickly.

She sneaks out of the school her usual way, through the window with the broken latch. A high stone wall, crumbling at the top, is all that lies between the school and the beach. She scrambles over it, using chunks of fallen rock as steps, and strolls as far as Shore

Road. She walks alongside the park to Atlantic Avenue, heading for the McDonald's. She has the allowance both parents put in her bank account. Plus she works a few hours filling in for absentees at the fish plant. If she runs short of money, there's always the dumpster behind the Food Mart where stuff ends up after the best-before date. Or she can hang around the back door of the Savage Harbour Inn, where Barlow Fist has a summer job in the kitchen. He'll always slip her a plate of something, even if it's only scraps.

Barlow is the only classmate who speaks to her. She smiles as she thinks of his solid build and thick shoulders, his gingery brown hair and freckled complexion, and the designer sunglasses he wears even when the sun's not out. She's surprised she's not invisible to someone like him. She knows he has a reputation. He hangs around with older kids who are out of school. Not kids, really. Men who don't seem to work, but always have plenty to spend. But Lettie doesn't care.

As she thinks of Barlow, she sees him walking across the park. She hopes he'll see her and wave, maybe even stop and talk. But he doesn't notice her. So she goes on her way to McDonald's.

Alone.

Chapter 5

Arn

The garbage can is such an easy target, Arn can't help himself. It's the town's fault for putting it there, on the corner of Seaside Park, beside a bench set back from the sidewalk on Atlantic Avenue. The shrubs at each end of the bench and the trees in the park behind make it a pretty private place to sit and think. Or a perfect place to show the people of Savage Harbour what you think of them and their town and their wonderful St. Isaac's School.

He tells Bilan, walking with him, "Let's sit for a bit."

He sprawls on the bench. Bilan sits upright beside him. He puts his arm behind her and pulls her towards him. She says, "Not here." He lifts a foot and rests it on the garbage can and pushes against it. He glances around. No pedestrians or cars in sight of the bench. He pushes harder.

Bilan says, "Arn, no."

Too late. It topples and falls. As it rolls across the sidewalk its contents spill out. Ice cream wrappers, lotto tickets, cigarette packets, coffee cups, tissues, Styrofoam take-out containers, and newspapers start to blow down Atlantic Avenue.

Arn laughs. "We better get out of here. Over the fence and through the park."

Bilan says, "Oh, sure." She looks down at her loose-fitting, russet-coloured pants drawn in at the ankle and her flimsy pink jacket with dangling ties. Her hijab is pink today.

Before she can protest, Arn picks her up and hugs her against his chest. She looks around wildly. He says, "Relax. No one can see." He wants to kiss her but knows that would totally freak her out. Every time he touches her, even if it's just holding hands, she's afraid someone will see and word will get back to her parents. He swings her easily over the fence and climbs after her.

She says, "I wish you wouldn't vandalise stuff like that."

He mumbles, "Not my fault."

They set off on one of the trails leading across the park to Shore Road. She lets him hold her hand while they're among the trees. They're on their way to their summer jobs. Bilan works for the same cleaning service as her mom, and the first home on their schedule is on Shore Road. Arn waits tables at Pete's Beach Café, at the end of Shore Road.

As they walk, Arn looks through the trees at the school he's been attending since he moved to Savage Harbour two years ago. A fresh start, his mom said, with his dad inside just for sharing a bit of dope. For anyone else it would've been a slap on the wrist, maybe a fine. But because it was Arn Saunders Senior, and he was black, it was two years in prison. Leaving Arn Junior to help his mom with the two little ones. No wonder Arn never "settled in" at St. Isaac's, never felt "accepted," like the guidance counsellor said he should. He never wanted to be settled in or accepted, anyway.

Bilan is the only reason Arn bothers going to school. He turns to look at her as they walk. She arrived in Savage Harbour around the same time as he did, struggling with the language, exotic and strange in a green hijab, with her brown skin and almond eyes and shining black hair. She was a magnet for the boys. A group of them moved in on her, Grant and Barlow among them. Arn doesn't know how he summoned the nerve but he blurted out, "She's with me." Of course, she wasn't.

Why would she be with someone like him?
The boys looked from Bilan to Arn. Barlow
sneered, "Yeah, right." But when they turned
back to Bilan, she looked at Arn and nodded
yes, and they backed off. And to his surprise
she's been with him ever since. She could have
anyone, with her smarts, and her cool, and her
looks. But she chose him. He still finds it hard
to believe.

He drags his eyes from her and looks back
at the school. He has plans for it. He's going to
break in. Smash the computers. Throw desks
and chairs around. Maybe even start a fire.
Then break as many windows as he can before
taking off. He just has to choose the right
night. He thinks he knows when that will be.

Bilan will be with him. She hasn't
abandoned him yet when he's in the mood for
a bit of harmless vandalism. She never does
anything herself, and always urges him to
stop. But she stays with him. He steels himself
against the day when she doesn't.

He sees Barlow Fist emerge from behind the school, looking like something spooked him. Their paths are on a collision course. As they pass, Barlow nods to Arn. But Arn is intent on watching him eye Bilan and smile at her.

When Barlow is out of earshot, Arn mutters, "Loser."

Bilan murmurs, "He is okay."

Arn looks at her quickly. Did she like that Barlow smiled at her? Did she smile back?

Chapter 6

Bilan

Bilan sees Arn looking at her. Knows Barlow smiling at her makes him jealous, although he has no reason to be. She tells Arn over and over that he's her boyfriend. She even lets him hold her hand and put his arm around her sometimes. She knows he wants more, much more, but she has this balancing act she has to maintain. It's not that her parents are so strict she's not allowed a boyfriend, just they don't like her to call Arn that. To them, he's her friend who just happens to be a boy. They even allow him to visit her when they're home. But they expect her to behave modestly, no public displays of affection. Holding hands might just about be okay, but certainly not kissing, or full body contact. She knows it drives Arn crazy.

She also knows he plans to vandalize St. Isaac's. She's lost count of how many times she's told him, "It is not worth it. You think it will make you feel better but it will not. And suppose we get caught."

She always says "we," determined to stay with him if he carries out his threat. She has stayed with him when he's done stupid stuff like tipping over the garbage can on Atlantic Avenue. She never joins in, just tries to restrain the anger that drives him to do it. She knows if they're caught her parents will be furious. They're anxious to be the "responsible citizens" they read about when they arrived in Canada after fleeing the revolution in Egypt.

Bilan is not sure why she's so determined

to stick by Arn. Is it because, while she hears anger in his voice, in his eyes she sees his hopes for the future fall apart? She saw the same frustration and despair in the eyes of her parents and their friends in Cairo. She wants to teach Arn acceptable means of expressing his anger, like with the demonstration she led. But that only resulted in him throwing the rock through the town hall window. He said afterwards he knew she'd be mad, but he didn't care because the Education Council deserved it. She agrees they did.

She squeezes his hand, trying to take his attention away from Barlow Fist, who smiled so nicely at her just now. He always does, so nicely that she can't help smiling back. She hopes Arn didn't see. She sneaks a glance after Barlow. He's near the main gate, where Grant Mograno is passing out pamphlets to tourists. Seeing her, Grant nods. Bilan waves and smiles without Arn seeing. Grant's a boy her parents would approve of. He's a good student, tall with blond hair neatly cut, smart in his navy blazer and khaki pants, good at sports.

The opposite of Arn.

Chapter 7

Grant

"We're going to miss the old place, aren't we?"

Grant starts. With a lull in the arrival of
visitors to Seaside Park, he was gazing down
the long central pathway to St. Isaac's. He
didn't hear his father approach until he spoke.

His father goes on without waiting for an
answer, "But now we're looking forward to new
challenges, aren't we?"

Grant answers in his head, *Like hell we are.*
He never contradicts his father. It doesn't

do any good. It's like his father doesn't hear. Besides, Grant knows it upsets his mother. So he's developed the habit of answering in what he calls his unspoken voice.

He goes on, in his head: *What you mean is, I'm supposed to look forward to new challenges whether I like it or not. And you expect me to cope with them, and still be the star student and athlete you think I've been all these years at St. Isaac's.*

And he knows he won't — can't — be the star his father wants him to be. He's simply not good enough, at school or at sports. He knows that's why he loved St. Isaac's. He's had the same classmates since primary school. Early on, he realized he could surpass them at his studies, as well as stand out in basketball and rugby, without being challenged. He knows it won't be the same next year at a bigger school. He's not as smart, not as good at sports as he's been led to believe. He'll no longer be a big fish. He knows he gets top marks only because most of his classmates just don't care.

And he knows his father, who chairs the Education Council, will be disappointed. Grant imagines he can hear the expectation of disappointment in his father's voice already.

Mr. Mograno pats Grant on the back. "I'm on my way to see an important client."

Important because he's got a shitload of money to invest.

"Just stopped by to say hello."

And to make sure I'm not making a mess of the job you got me with the Town.

Grant watches his father drive away. He couldn't care less about doing what his father expects, like going to university and getting a degree in finance before joining his investment company. Grant has no intention of doing any of that, but he hasn't gathered the nerve to tell his father. Not yet. Not until he can leave home.

Grant turns away from the road and looks back towards St. Isaac's. He sees Arn and

Bilan crossing the park. He nods to Bilan after making sure Arn isn't looking, and is stupidly thrilled when she smiles and gives a little wave. He'd like to ask her out, but hasn't got the nerve, knowing he'd have Arn to contend with. Plus she's so smart and confident and pretty that he's intimidated by her. It should make her look strange, the way she dresses in her Egyptian clothes, with not a stitch of skin showing except her face. But it's a total turn on. He can't understand it.

He watches her for as long as she's in sight, trying not to make it too obvious. Then he shifts his gaze to his former school. He'd like to pay it a last visit and find something to take from it, to remember it by. He thinks he knows how to get in, and a good time to do it.

A discarded *Atlantic Daily News* lies on a bench nearby. He picks it up and reads:

ST. ISAAC'S SCHOOL TO CLOSE

Savage Harbour's hundred-year-old St. Isaac's School, whose graceful façade serves as both a backdrop and a central feature of Seaside Park, and which serves the senior high students of the town, is to close at the end of this school year. Its ninety-five students will be bussed thirty-five kilometres to the provincial capital of Laneyville, where they will attend Laneyville Central High School.

Grant is mad that the first they heard of their school closing was the gossip spreading through town after the June District Education Council meeting. Then the politicians and the parents and the community all got in the act. They had their say in letters to the newspaper and at public meetings and at more Education Council meetings.

But no one thought to ask the kids.

The only action students had time for was the walk out and march to the town hall. Grant joined in because his fear of losing face with other students was greater than his fear of what his father would, and did, say. The next day, the principal demanded to know who threw the rock. No one would tell, although Arn volunteered to own up. They were all suspended for two days. When the principal announced it, with Mr. Kitchener scowling beside him, Arn and Barlow and a few others laughed out loud at being barred from school for not being in school.

Those were the last two days of term, a fine end to his time at St. Isaac's. For a moment, before he pushes the feelings away, Grant understands the anger that drives Arn to his silly acts of vandalism. He even feels like doing some vandalism himself. What are you supposed to do when you're overlooked and ignored?

Chapter 8

Breaking In

Lettie

Asleep in a chair in the staff room, Lettie starts at the sound of a loud pop, like a cork coming out of a gigantic bottle. It's followed by another, louder, pop.

The windowless room is in total darkness. Still half asleep, she doesn't know where she is. Maybe in bed at home. Then she remembers. Her father is nearly 5,000 kilometres away in one direction, her mother 1,500 kilometres in the opposite direction.

And she's alone.

Usually it doesn't bother her. She's used to it. She keeps busy during weekends and holidays with a routine of walking, eating, reading, and working to replace the routine imposed by school. But nights are difficult. The silence closing in on her forces her to ask, *Will it always be like this? Will I still be alone when I'm old? Will I leave the TV on all the time for company? Will I talk back to it? Will I seize on casual conversation at the grocery store checkout and have to be ushered out as the lineup grows behind me? Will I sit alone in Tim Horton's making one cup of coffee last as long as I can, and try to ignore customers who look at me half pitying, half scornful, like it's my fault I'm on my own?*

Will I ever have a boyfriend? How do you go about getting one, anyway?

A crackling sound and a long, drawn out explosion, like thunder, break into her thoughts. She realizes what's going on. It's

Savage Harbour's annual Goodbye to Summer firework display on the Friday before the new school term.

The fireworks are set off over the sea. The crowds that gather on the beaches and the wharves to watch keep the police busy and leave the streets empty, like a ghost town. She decides to climb over the seawall and watch from the beach behind the school, well away from the crowds.

She's groping her way across the staff room when, through a barrage of crackles and explosions, she hears a noise that doesn't belong with the fireworks. It's a kind of scraping from the classroom next door. She freezes, listening. Another scrape, and a scratching sound, followed by a thud, like something heavy dropped on the floor. Someone's breaking in. She doesn't want to get trapped in the staff room with nowhere to hide and no way of escape. But before she can move there's the crash of a chair tipped over and an exclamation, "Shit." A giggle.

Lettie opens the door and peers out, listening. She hears a bump and a shuffle. She has to sneak past the classroom where the sounds are coming from to find a new hiding place. She inches her way to the classroom door and peers around it. A sliver of light shines into the room from the security light at the corner of the school. It's just enough for her to make out an open window and the shapes of two people.

Bilan and Arn

A rocket explodes over the sea in a cascading shower of streaming sparks. Bilan and Arn stand in the flickering light that briefly fills the classroom. Another rocket flares and Bilan sees someone hovering near the door.

She gasps, "Lettie, what are you doing here?"

Lettie manages, "I . . ."

Arn cuts her off. "Whatever you're up to,

Lettie, keep out of our way. We've got plans for the school tonight."

Bilan glares at him. "You mean *you* have plans." She looks back at Lettie. "Why are you here?"

"I . . . I live here. S-sometimes."

Bilan sighs, "Oh, Lettie."

Arn shakes his head and mutters, "Jesus. Poor kid."

Bilan turns to Arn. "Now what are you going to do? Wreck poor Lettie's home?"

Footsteps sound in the hallway, coming closer. Lettie hurries into the classroom and crouches behind a desk with Arn and Bilan.

Bilan glances at Lettie, crouched beside her. She sees Lettie blinking rapidly and tapping her fingers together in a kind of fingertip dance. Bilan puts a hand on her shoulder to calm her while they peer through the desks between them and the classroom door.

Grant

Grant Mograno walks past in the hallway, shining a small flashlight on the ground. Bilan looks at Arn, eyebrows raised. He shrugs, finger to lips. Grant reappears. He stares into the classroom. Flashes the light over the open window. Starts towards it.

Arn stands. Bilan and Lettie do the same.

Grant stops, gaping, as his flashlight catches them. "Holy shit, where did you all come from?"

Arn says, "Put the friggin' light off and tell us what you're doing here."

"Nothing."

"Nothing like hell. How'd you get in?"

"Kind of borrowed a key from my dad. Principal left it with him, just in case. I've got to get it back before Dad misses it."

"So piss off out of here. And take Lettie with you."

"You can't tell me . . ."

Bilan interrupts. "Ssssh."

They stare at one another as more footsteps approach in the hallway. In the dim light Bilan notices Lettie's eyes flutter and her fingertips dancing again. She takes her hand and squeezes it gently, stilling her fingers.

Barlow

Barlow strolls into the classroom, talking on his cell phone.

Arn starts, "What . . ."

Barlow holds up one finger while he finishes his call. "It's off. Too risky. Maybe try another night. I'll explain later." He puts the phone away and takes out a small flashlight. "Hi, guys. Is this a party or what?"

Bilan shields her eyes as he plays the light briefly over her face. He smiles at her as he lowers it. She wants to smile back, but Arn is watching. Barlow moves the flashlight on to Lettie, and says, "How ya doing, Let?" He snaps the light off as he nods to Arn and Grant.

Bilan says, "You scared Lettie."

Barlow looks at Lettie. "Did I, Let? Sorry. Didn't mean to."

Arn snarls, "How'd you get in?"

"Through the same window as you. Couple of hours ago. I took a look around. Peeked in on you, Lettie. You were sound asleep. Didn't even stir when I shone the flashlight on you." He winks at her. "You looked some cute."

Even in the dim light Bilan sees Lettie blush. She says, "Leave her alone."

"Whoa. Sorry again."

"I can guess what you're doing here," says Arn. "Looks like we spoiled your plans."

"And I can guess what you're here for. You better put that off until another night, when I'm through with my work here."

"Screw you. By the time I've finished there'll be nothing left for you. And there's piss all you can do about it."

"You're not hearing me, Arn. You're not getting up to any of your tricks here until I'm done. Then you can do what you like."

Arn moves towards Barlow. He mutters, "I'm going to . . ."

Barlow notices Lettie's fingers flying and holds up his hand, halting Arn. "Shit. Sorry, Lettie," he says.

Grant says, "You're crazy, both of you. All of you. I'm outta here."

"First you better say what you came for," says Arn.

"Nothing to do with you," says Grant.

"Wanna bet?" says Arn.

Chapter 9
One Plan

Listening to the boys squabble, Bilan feels a familiar lurch of fear in her stomach. She's back in Tahrir Square, standing among her parents and their friends. They're arguing about their next move as the military moves in. Voices grow louder and gestures fiercer. Their disagreement threatens to turn them against one another and destroy their unity.

She puts her hands on her hips and glares

at the boys. "Stop your stupid bickering, the three of you."

The cascading light of a rocket streams through the room. Bilan sees Lettie slump into a desk. She rests her elbows on it and lowers her head into her hands.

Bilan goes on, quieter, "Why do we not all say what we are doing here? Because I think at bottom we are here for the same reason."

"Barlow doesn't have to say. He's going to clean the place out," says Arn. "Steal everything he can. Him and his no good brother."

"Seemed like a good night for the job, with everyone at the fireworks, including the police. Until you showed up," says Barlow. He levels his finger at Arn. "And I know you broke in thinking you'd do a bit of damage — right?"

Arn mutters, "I'm going to tear this effin' dump apart. I'm going to show everyone how I feel about St. Isaac's. How I feel about all the times you and the teachers looked down on me and treated me like shit."

"When did I ever treat you like shit?"
Grant protests. "I hardly ever speak to you."

"Right."

"But that's just because we've never been,
like, friends."

"Wonder why," Arn scoffs. "Wouldn't
have anything to do with my dad being inside,
would it? I bet your folks told you not to have
anything to do with that Saunders family that
moved into town."

Even in the dim light Bilan sees Grant
colour up and knows it's true.

"So why don't you tell us what you're up
to, Grant?" says Barlow.

"Told you — nothing to do with you."

"Spill it, Grant," says Arn. "Or I'll choke it
out of you."

Grant looks down at his feet. Shuffles
them. "Just thought I'd get something to, like,
remember the old place by. Maybe the plaque
with the school motto from the hallway, or one
of the banners from the gym."

"Like a souvenir of the good times," Arn scoffs. "You're sick."

Bilan says slowly, "What you are all planning is really a protest over the school closing. None of us wants anything to change. I have already had enough upheaval to last me a lifetime. And you do not want to change schools, Arn. Despite what you say about hating St. Isaac's, you are afraid you will feel even more out of place at Laneyville."

A firework shoots a series of white balls of fire over the sea behind the school. They explode into colour as they arc and drift slowly down. The students' faces reflect red, yellow, and green in turn as they stare at Arn, who murmurs, "You have to wear a uniform at Laneyville, a blazer and a school tie and a white shirt and crap like that. And no jeans." He turns to Bilan. "And you'll have to wear a white blouse and a green sweater and a grey skirt. Do you seriously think you're going to get away with wearing your hijab and your long dresses and stuff?"

"We will see," says Bilan quietly.

She walks to where Lettie sits. Bilan lifts Lettie's hands from her face. "And you do not want the school to close either. We are all used to how you are, but at Laneyville you will have to start all over again, with the students not understanding you."

Lettie murmurs, "Th-thinking I'm a f-freak."

"We don't think that," says Arn. "Never have. Never would."

Bilan turns on Grant. "And you do not want the school to close because you are scared of going to Laneyville, too."

"Scared of what?"

"Of finding out you're not as smart as you've been told. And you won't be the sports superstar you are here," says Barlow. "And Daddy won't be pleased, will he?"

Grant mumbles, "Piss off, Barlow."

"That leaves you, Barlow," says Bilan. "Why are you really here?"

"You mean apart from making a bundle of money?" He shrugs. "Simple. I want the school to stay open because I don't want Savage Harbour to change."

"How's the town going to change?" says Grant.

"The school's always the first thing to go in a dying town. It's like taking the heart out of a place. Next it's the post office. Then the bus into town. After that no young families move in because there's no school. That means the businesses close because they got no workers, followed by the stores because no one's got any money to spend in them. Soon you're in Deadsville. Nothing left except empty churches falling down and a bunch of sad old people whining about how things aren't what they used to be."

"Where'd you get all this stuff?" Arn asks.

"My dad works for the town. He worries about losing his job because it's dying. My family's been here since my great grandad and

Dad says it'd be a shame for us to have to leave after all these years."

Bilan asks, "So do you — all of you — feel strongly enough about the school closing to try to stop it? Instead of wrecking it, or stealing from it, or taking souvenirs."

"You mean, like, protest?" says Arn.

She says slowly, her eyes never leaving his, "I mean protest in a legitimate way."

"Suppose we did protest," says Barlow. "Would the other kids join us?"

"We'd have to find out fast," says Arn. "Like this weekend, before school starts on Monday."

"We could spread the word by talking to students and asking them to pass it on," says Bilan.

"They'll blab," says Arn. "Word will get out."

Barlow grins. "Not if we threaten them."

"If that is what it takes," says Bilan. "And tell them to put nothing on social media. We have to keep everything secret at least long enough to start the protest. Just ask if they want to join, without telling the plan."

"But what is the plan?" Grant asks. "The last one, the march to the town hall, didn't do any good, did it?"

"First — are we all in?"

She looks in turn at Arn, Barlow, Grant, and Lettie. They nod one by one.

A huge explosion roars in from the sea and rolls over the school into the park. It echoes from the trees and rumbles back and forth until it dies away. A few seconds later they hear distant cheering and applause.

"So here is the plan," says Bilan.

Chapter 10

Spreading the Word

Arn

"Hey, kids," says Arn. "Heard the news?"

The five middle school boys leaving the Dollar Store with gum and suckers look at him warily. He grins, knowing he has a reputation and enjoying it. On Saturday morning he has nothing to do now that the Beach Café's closed for the winter and his shift at the grocery store doesn't start until noon.

"Like any news you got is worth hearing," says one.

Arn laughs. He remembers the student's name. Mitchell. He makes a sudden movement with his hand as if to hit him. Mitchell recoils. Then he realises it was just a feint, and grins. Arn says, "There's going to be a protest about the school closing and us having to go to Laneyville Central."

"Why?" says Mitchell.

"What d'you mean — why?"

"Why the protest? It's going to be great, going to Laneyville."

"Like how?"

"Like being in the city every day. And hanging out downtown after school. Better than being stuck in Savage Harbour."

"And those city girls," says another of the students.

"What do you know about city girls?" says Arn. "They eat little kids like you alive." He looks the group over. No protesters here. "Well

if that's how you feel . . . If you change your
mind be at school at eight o'clock Monday,
instead of getting the bus to Laneyville. You
can pass it on to your friends. But don't let on
to anyone like teachers or parents. And nothing
on Facebook and stuff."

"Says who?" Mitchell challenges.

"Me," says Arn.

Mitchell smirks.

Arn adds, "Me and Barlow."

The kids look at one another.

Mitchell says, "Okay."

Lettie

She steels herself to speak. "E-excuse me."
Lettie knows she's blinking like crazy but can't
stop it.

Lauralee, Chelsea, and Sharlane don't seem
to hear. They're wearing new clothes, and their
hair is teased and styled in a way it never was
at St. Isaac's. They're gazing into the window of
Karen's Klothes on Water Street. A mannequin

is dressed in the girls' uniform of Laneyville Central High School. It wears the grey knee-length skirt, white blouse, green sweater, and straw boater hat with a green ribbon. A notice beside it proclaims, *Available Here. Exclusively!*

Lauralee says, "It's so cool."

"Imagine us walking around Laneyville dressed like that," Chelsea breathes.

"Yeah — not just in jeans and sweatshirts and stuff," Sharlane adds. "We'll be like models."

"Hitch the skirt up a few centimetres, undo a couple of buttons, and we'll be boy magnets," Lauralee adds.

"And we can accessorize, right?" says Chelsea. "I'm going to accessorize with a big label. It's going to say — I'm available!"

They collapse in giggles.

Lettie repeats, "E-excuse me."

Her eyes are still aflutter. Now she can feel her thumbs tapping her fingers one after the other. She taps thumb and first finger, thumb and second finger, thumb and third finger, thumb and fourth finger. Then she starts again, over and over, both hands.

She catches the rolling of eyes that passes among her classmates. Then Lauralee says, in a singsong voice as if she's speaking to a toddler, "Hi, Lettie. What's up?"

"There's . . . There's going to be a . . . a k-kind of . . . p-protest," Lettie starts. "D-don't get the bus on M-Monday. M-meet at the s-school instead."

Getting the words out is agony. She wouldn't have joined the protest if she knew she'd have to talk about it. She thought of not passing on the news, then lying to the others that she had. But she decided that would be wrong.

"You . . . You should . . . You can j-join if you don't w-want St. Isaac's to close. If you think we shouldn't h-have to go to Laneyville."

She is blinking and her fingers are doing their frantic dance.

"Never heard you talk so much, Lettie,"
says Lauralee.

"You've got yourself all worked up about it,
haven't you?" says Chelsea.

"What's not to like about going to
Laneyville?" says Lauralee. "We don't all want
to hide ourselves away in Savage Harbour."

She doesn't have to say, *Like you.*

"They say there's three boys for every girl
at the school," says Chelsea. "I can't decide if
I'll have three at the same time or go through
them one after the other."

"You mean they'll go through you one
after the other," Sharlane puts in. The girls fall
against one another, laughing.

"Imagine that, Lettie," says Lauralee. "All
those boys. You might even get lucky yourself."

They move off down the street.

Lettie calls after them, "P . . . Please tell
any students you see about the p-protest. But
it's a secret for only students. Y-you're . . .
You're not to tell any adults or t-teachers."

They stop and turn. Lauralee sticks her hip out and plants her hand on it. "Oh yeah. Who says we're not to tell?"

"M-me," says Lettie.

More eye rolling and they laugh again.

"B-Barlow says it, t-too," Lettie adds.

The girls glance at one another. Lauralee says, "Okay then."

Lettie watches them continue down the street. She's breathing quickly as if she's been running. But at least her blinking is slowing and her fingers are still.

She hears, "Taking my name in vain?"

She turns. She didn't hear Barlow coming up behind her.

"S-sorry," she says. "I d-didn't know w-what else to say. They d-don't l-listen to me."

"You'd be surprised," says Barlow. "How are you making out, anyway?"

"I've s-spoken to about a dozen k-kids, all g-grades," says Lettie. "No one s-seems interested in joining a p-protest."

"Same here," says Barlow. "But you never know. They might change their minds. And who knows how the others are doing. Let's take a break and get a coffee."

Lettie says, "I . . . er . . . I . . ."

She knows you're supposed to talk if you have coffee with someone. But she won't know what to say. And if she does find something to say, it'll come out stupid. It always does. That's why it's always best to stay silent.

Barlow prompts, "What?"

"I . . . er . . ."

"You gotta be somewhere. That's okay. Another time, eh?"

"N-no," says Lettie. "Y-yes."

Barlow grins. "No you don't want a coffee and yes you gotta be somewhere? Or no you haven't gotta be somewhere and yes you do want a coffee?"

"A c-coffee," says Lettie. "P-please."

"Relax," says Barlow. "I'm only asking you if you want a coffee, not if you want to marry me."

Lettie blushes furiously and hopes Barlow doesn't notice.

They sit in Harbour Java on Water Street. Barlow gets two coffees.

Lettie says, "I'll . . . I'll pay."

Barlow says, "Save your money."

They sit in silence, watching people passing on the street.

Eventually, Lettie murmurs, "S-sorry."

"What for?"

She looks down, stirring her coffee. "I d-don't talk m-much."

"You don't say."

She looks up.

Barlow is grinning again. Or smiling. What's the difference, anyway? And does it matter?

He says, "No problem. I like silence."

A few students come and go. Lettie likes how they notice her sitting with Barlow, as he beckons them over and tells them about the protest. She envies the ease and confidence with which he does it. But they seem no more interested in protesting than the students she's spoken to. Barlow ends each conversation with, "You can tell other students, but no one else. No one. Got it? If you do, I'll hear about it — and you'll answer to me."

Lettie ventures, "Do . . . Do you suppose anyone will tell on us?"

Barlow shrugs. "Who cares? Word's bound to get out sooner or later."

"W-what happens then?" says Lettie.

Barlow grins again. Or smiles. "That's when the fun begins."

Grant

Grant is alone at home on Sunday night when the phone rings. It's the day before the new school term and the protest. He peers at the call display. Stafford Kitchener. The arsehole superintendent of schools.

Grant's father tells him to always answer the phone with 'Mograno Investments', so

Grant says, "Yo."

A beat.

Then: "Mograno?"

"Grant. His son."

"You sound like your father. Mr. Kitchener here. Do I know you?"

Grant's unspoken voice starts up. *Of course you know me, dickhead. You suspended me for two days for protesting about the school closing.*

He says aloud, "I don't think so."

Silence at the other end, as if Grant is expected to say more. He tries, "Sir."

It seems to satisfy Mr. Kitchener. "Are you in high school?"

Grant holds the phone away from his ear. Mr. Kitchener doesn't so much talk as bark.

"Yes, sir. Grade eleven. Going into grade twelve."

"At Laneyville Central. You must be excited about the move. I know your father is."

"Yes, sir." *I'm pissing myself with excitement. Sir.*

Mr. Kitchener is right about Grant's father, who is all for the move to Laneyville Central. He says Grant will meet a better class of student there and make contacts that will serve him well after university.

"Is your father in, Grant?"

"No. Can I give him a message?"

Silence.

"Sir."

"Ask him what's going on down there."

Grant thinks, *Shit. The news is out already. I wonder who blabbed.* He asks cautiously, "Like what, sir?"

"I hear rumours about a student revolt in Savage Harbour over St. Isaac's closing. Have you heard anything?"

"Not a thing, sir." *Like I'd tell you, arsehole.*

"I'm not surprised. I wouldn't expect Mograno's boy to know anything about that kind of foolishness. If there's any truth in it, it'll be the work of a few renegades and malcontents."

Count me among them, butthead.

"It's probably not worth taking any notice of. But I think your father should know about it. You might keep your ear to the ground yourself, and let me know if you hear anything."

"Of course, sir." *Up yours, sir.*

He scribbles a message for his father. *Mr. Kitchener called. Wants to know what's going on down here.* He can pretend to be asleep when his parents get home. And he'll make sure he's out early to avoid any questions from his father.

He wonders whether to call the others and tell them the word is out. Decides not to. There's nothing they can do about it. They knew it would happen sooner or later.

And they certainly aren't about to cancel their plan.

Chapter 11

Time To Occupy

Eight o'clock Monday, a grey, windy morning, Lettie waits by the big glass doors in the wood-panelled entrance hall of the school, ready to open them as arranged. But no one is there.

She's been awake since five, and slept only fitfully until then, imagining what would happen when the protest was discovered. What sort of punishments would they receive? Would they be lined up at Laneyville Central to be berated by Mr. Kitchener? She remembers his silent, glowering presence when they were all suspended. She can imagine his anger. She couldn't face it. She'd have to take off. Disappear.

She peers across The Meadows to the woods. Still no sign of anyone and it's nearly ten after eight. She knew they wouldn't come. The enticing thought of the friendship she might have found by joining the movement was just a tease. It looks like she'll be the only one protesting. It's too late to get the bus to Laneyville Central, but she can start tomorrow without too many questions being asked.

Or maybe it's time to move on, and not bother with school. She's good at disappearing. She's not sure she can face starting over at Laneyville, even with the others as maybe, kind of friends after Friday night. She suspects they'd soon discover lots of new friends, anyway.

She's so lost in thought she doesn't see Arn and Bilan scurry through the trees and across The Meadows. Bilan taps on the door and Lettie opens it and they rush in, a swirl of wind following them.

Bilan hugs Lettie and says, "It is time to occupy!"

Lettie confesses, "I . . . I thought no one would come."

She looks back into the park and sees Barlow, hands in pockets, strolling across The Meadows. How should she greet him after their coffee together on Saturday? He'd left her outside Harbour Java with a smile and a wink and, "See you Monday, Let." Was that enough to make them more than friends?

She opens the door for him and he says, "Hiya, Lettie. You look like shit."

"Barlow!" says Bilan.

Lettie feels a rush of embarrassment. How could she think they might be more than friends? She wishes she could be alone. It was easier.

"What I mean is, Lettie looks seriously worried," Barlow explains. He turns back to Lettie. "You hardly slept last night, right?"

"R-right."

"You got nothing to worry about," says Barlow. "Whatever happens with our protest, we're all in it together. So we all look out for one another."

He smiles at her. And pats her arm. He smiles at everyone, she reminds herself quickly, especially the girls. Especially Bilan. But he smiled at her in a different way. *Didn't he?*

Arn looks out the door and says, "Here's Grant, looking like a turkey."

Grant is skulking through the trees in his Laneyville Central uniform. He pauses at the edge of The Meadows and looks around — needlessly, because no one's there. Then he runs to the door. As Lettie opens it, he announces breathlessly, "I had to pretend I was going to Laneyville. My father came to the bus stop to see the first bus run, playing at being Mr. Important Chair of the Education Council. Only way I got here was his cell phone rang. While he was talking on it I kinda drifted away from the kids waiting for the bus and wandered into the park like I was just strolling around, and when the bus came I ducked behind some shrubs and then took off. Some of the kids may have seen me, but it doesn't matter. Word's out already. Kitchener called my dad last night. He wanted to know what was going on down here in Savage Harbour, like it's some kind of backwoods colony of Laneyville."

"But he does not know what we are going to do — right?" says Bilan.

"Don't think so. Not yet."

"Doesn't look like anyone else is joining us," says Barlow, watching outside.

"Never thought they would, from the time we started putting the word around," says Arn.

"Same here," Grant adds. "Looks like it's just the five of us."

"The Gang of Five!" says Bilan. "That is what we will call ourselves."

"What are we going to do if there's just us?" says Arn.

"We will do exactly what we planned," says Bilan. "So let us get on with the protest."

Lettie makes sure the door is locked. With their footsteps echoing through the empty school they walk through the locker-lined hallways to their old classroom at the back of the building.

Arn stops at the door and says, "I still think we should smash up at least a classroom or two. Just to let them know how we feel."

"Be sensible," says Barlow. "We can get around a thousand dollars for the computers and stuff in this classroom alone. Why don't we stick a few of them out the back, then I'll call my brother, and . . ."

Without thinking, Lettie stamps her foot and says, "N-no!"

The other four stare at her and she mutters, "S-sorry."

"Lettie is right," says Bilan. "We agreed — no stealing or vandalizing, and no souvenirs. We have to make sure that when they discover us all we are doing is carrying on with our studies in our old school. You choose what you want to work on. All our books are still here, and we help one another. When someone in authority arrives — and someone will — we have to be sure they have no reason for accusing us of doing anything wrong. That includes being rude to them."

"But who's going to do the talking when they come?" says Arn. "Better not be me if we can't be rude."

"You should speak for us, Bilan, because you've, like, been through a revolution. Our protest must be small potatoes to you," says Grant.

"Injustice — and that is what we are facing here — is never small potatoes. It always has to be challenged," says Bilan.

Lettie thinks she sounds like a revolutionary, like someone she's seen in movies. She wonders what kind of trouble Bilan will lead them into.

Chapter 12

In It Together

Barlow

At noon, they take a break and get out their packed lunches. Lettie leaves the classroom. Barlow waits a few minutes, then goes looking for her, taking his lunch with him. He finds her in the staff room and says, "You got no food — right?"

She shrugs. "It's okay. I usually skip lunch, anyway."

"That's what I thought," he says, and offers her a sandwich.

She says, "I'm not eating your lunch."

"You're not," says Barlow. "I brought extra."

He feels like he did when he asked her if she wanted a coffee. He wonders why he's doing it, and why it gives him such a jolt of pleasure to give her a cheese sandwich on week-old bread. He feels like slapping himself, to bring himself back to the real world, where a cup of coffee and a cheese sandwich mean . . . a cup of coffee and a cheese sandwich. Nothing more.

When they've all finished lunch, they go to the gym and play basketball. Barlow and Arn coach Lettie, who's never played before. Lettie, running backwards to catch the ball, trips and stumbles towards Barlow, who's standing behind her. He puts his arms out to catch her. His hands land on her hips and slide upwards to her waist as she regains her balance. She half turns to him, biting her lip as she breathes, "Th-thank you."

While Arn goes to the washroom, Barlow and Lettie take a break. They sit on the bleachers watching Grant and Bilan, who have drifted to the other end of the gym to practise shooting. Several times during the morning, Barlow watched as Grant asked Bilan about a current affairs essay he was working on. And twice Grant sat with her while she explained something. Now he's standing close beside her, demonstrating how to shoot while she copies his actions. When she shoots and misses Grant says, "Like this." He stands behind her and takes her hands in his. He moves them in the action of shooting with his arms around her. He says, "Got it?" and stands closer, brushing against her.

Arn returns without them noticing. He pads silently and quickly past Barlow and Lettie until he's behind Grant. He spins him round by the shoulder. Lettie half rises. Barlow murmurs, "Relax," as he saunters up the gym.

"Getting a good feel?" Arn asks Grant.

"Just shooting baskets," says Grant.

"Shooting your load more like," says Arn.

Bilan gasps, "Arn!"

Arn grabs Grant by the shirt and hauls him close. Barlow steps between them and tells Grant, "Go take a cold shower."

Grant slinks from the gym.

Bilan starts, "Arn, he was just . . ."

Arn ignores her and stalks to the side of the gym, where he throws himself on the bleachers. Bilan goes to follow, but Barlow steers her up the gym where Lettie is sitting. They take seats beside her.

Barlow says, "Give him a minute to calm down. Then go talk to him, and everything will be okay."

She starts, "I should not have . . ."

Barlow interrupts. "Don't blame yourself. It's not your fault." Then he leans close to her and adds, "You can't help it you're cute."

Bilan looks at him quickly. He grins and she pushes him away, laughing.

As he speaks, he thinks, *This is how you talk to girls. You tease them and flirt with them. It means nothing but they love it, although they'll never admit it. This is the real me, not the stranger practically getting a hard-on from watching a skinny girl eat a cheese sandwich.*

Barlow watches Bilan walk slowly back to where Arn is sitting on the bleachers. Arn looks away, but she sits with him and soon they're talking quietly. Barlow turns to Lettie. She's not there. He looks around. She's almost running from the gym. He mutters to himself, "What's wrong with her?" Then he finds he can still feel the unexpected firmness of her hips under his hands as he caught her. He realizes he hasn't really thought of her as having body parts before.

Lettie

She hurries back to the classroom and tackles a difficult math problem. Anything to drive the sight of Barlow smiling at Bilan from her mind. She knows she has no right to be jealous. He owes her nothing. She means nothing to him. But she can't help it.

After a few minutes, he walks in with Grant. She hears Barlow say, as they head for their desks, "So cool it, man. At least while it's just the five of us in this thing together." Arn and Bilan follow ten minutes later. They're holding hands and their faces are flushed. Arn's shirt is hanging out.

Halfway through the afternoon Lettie hears a sharp click. She looks up from her math book. No one else seems to have heard. If the click is followed by a scrape it means someone is opening the front door. She knows the sounds well. If she heard them when she stayed at the school during term, it meant she'd overslept. The custodian on early shift was arriving and she had to move fast and hide. She hears the squeak of Barlow's pen, the murmur of Arn and Bilan discussing a book, the tapping of Grant's fingers on his desk. He's watching them — watching Bilan — while he pretends to read.

Then a scrape.

Lettie whispers urgently, "S-someone's coming."

She stands, ready to run and hide. She pictures police storming the school, handcuffing them, bundling them into vans.

Bilan quietly closes the door and says, "Keep working. Let me do the talking."

Footsteps in the hallway. Men's voices.

Grant mutters, "Shit. It's my father."

Lettie sits with her head over her book but her eyes on the door. Her hands are shaking. She feels cold but she's sweating. The door bursts open and Mr. Mograno marches in. She thinks he looks like Grant will look in twenty years. He has the same blond hair but darker and thinning, same athletic build but gone saggy, same face but fleshier. He wears a dark grey suit and white shirt and red tie. Another man follows him. Mr. Kitchener. He wears a suit, too, but his is dark blue. They look like Jehovah's Witnesses. But Jehovah's Witnesses are never angry.

Mr. Kitchener charges to the front of the room and stands with his arms folded, glaring at the students. Mr. Mograno stands over Grant's desk and says, "I had a call from the principal of Laneyville Central. He said five Savage Harbour students, one of them you, failed to report to school this morning. The bus driver reported seeing two or three students heading through the park in the direction of the old school. What's going on? What do you think you're doing?"

Bilan stands and starts, "We, the Gang of Five, are protesting . . ."

Mr. Mograno interrupts. "I didn't ask you."

"But I am the agreed spokesperson for the group, so I will answer. We, the Gang of Five, are protesting . . ."

Mr. Kitchener explodes with, "The

Gang of Five. The *Gang of Five*. What sort of nonsense is . . ."

Bilan cuts him off. "Please let me continue. We, the Gang of Five, are occupying St. Isaac's School to protest . . ."

Mr. Kitchener, his face red and his hands now by his side with fists clenched, barks, "Just who do you think you are, to speak to me like that?"

Lettie shrinks into her seat as Bilan's voice rises. "We are protesting the decision by the Education Council to close our school. It was a decision that, shamefully, we were never consulted on and never even learned about until the last few weeks of term. We understand that the school district faces financial challenges. But we do not agree that having Savage Harbour students attend Laneyville Central is the best way of solving them."

Lettie thinks that Bilan sounds like a person in power, and that Mr. Kitchener sounds like a bully as he spits, "Now you listen to me, young lady. You are students. Therefore you have obligations, not rights. And one of them is to obey your superiors."

"You mean adults in arbitrary positions of authority. We acknowledge no obligation to obey them."

Now Lettie thinks Bilan sounds like a rebel. She's proud of Bilan's defiance and of herself for standing with her. But she fears the anger their protest is already bringing down on them.

Mr. Kitchener strides to Bilan and stands over her, more like a bully than ever. Lettie is afraid he's going to hit her. "You will stop trespassing on school property. You will end your so-called occupation immediately. And you will report to Laneyville Central High tomorrow morning."

Bilan says calmly, "I will consult with the group. Together we will decide our course of action."

Mr. Kitchener looks like he's going to have

a heart attack. His face grows even redder and he roars, "If you defy me and continue your illegal occupation, you will suffer the severest punishment the District can impose."

He turns and stomps from the room.

Mr. Mograno growls at Grant, "Are you coming?"

Grant shakes his head.

"Then I'll talk to you at home." He follows the superintendent out.

Bilan calls after them, "Thank you for visiting us." As soon as they've gone, she falls back into her chair. She takes a deep breath and exhales, "Whew."

Lettie, shaking and wringing her hands, thinks she's going to throw up.

They sit in silence until Barlow says, "Whoa. Heavy." He looks around the room. Grins at Lettie. "Okay, everybody. They're gone and we're cool. Nice work, Madam Spokesperson. What now?"

Bilan pulls herself up in her chair and

takes another deep breath. "Now we work for another hour, just as we planned."

Barlow moves to sit beside Lettie. He whispers, "Okay?"

She nods as she tries to control her dancing fingers.

He pushes his chair back and settles down to read with his feet on his desk.

At three o'clock Bilan mutters, "See you tomorrow," and leaves with Arn and Grant.

Barlow reads on.

Lettie looks at him from the corner of her eyes. "Aren't you going?"

Barlow grins. "Thought you might like company for a while, after the Invasion of the Dickheads. Then maybe you can come to the inn while I work. When I finish I'll find us something to eat, then walk you back here. Or you can home with me."

Lettie whispers, "Oh."

Barlow says, "So — how about it?"

Chapter 13

Renegades

Grant

Mr. Mograno paces in the room he calls his study, hands behind his back.

"Let's consider who you have in your so called Gang of Five." He ticks them off on his fingers as he goes on. "A thief and a vandal, both known to police. A silly, brainless flake of a girl. And an immigrant, who should be grateful for the opportunity of attending a fine school in a civilized country instead of a hut in the bush. Instead she abuses the privileges offered her. How much credibility do you think you have? And what are you doing with people like them?"

Grant stands before his father, hands in pockets, slouching because he knows it makes his father crazy. He shrugs. "They're my friends."

"Friends! I thought I'd brought you up with better judgement."

Mrs. Mograno, standing behind her husband, tells Grant, "Listen to your father, dear."

Mr. Mograno stops pacing and glares at Grant. "Take your hands out of your pockets when I'm talking to you."

Grant obeys, then returns his hands to his pockets. He can't remember ever defying his father before today. Now he's done it twice within a few hours, first at the school when he refused to leave, and now by keeping his hands in his pockets. Like it matters somehow.

Defiance is becoming a habit. He doesn't know whether he's exhilarated or frightened. He thinks he likes it. He feels like he no longer needs his unspoken voice.

Mr. Mograno stares at him. Shakes his head. "I don't know what's got into you. I'll expect you to come to your senses in the morning. You will end this foolishness, attend Laneyville Central, and leave your misguided renegade friends to their fate. In any case, keep clear of St. Isaac's in the morning. Mr. Kitchener is calling the police as soon as he hears of any illegal entry to the school."

Mrs. Mograno is crying.

"If my friends are renegades then so am I," Grant says, feeling proud.

"Then I'll see you in police custody. And don't expect any sympathy. Carry on like this for much longer and you may find you no longer have a home."

Grant mutters, "Okay."

He's not worried. He has somewhere to

go. Before they left the school, Bilan asked him quietly, "Will you be in serious trouble with your father?"

He said, not sure he believed himself, "Nothing I can't handle."

"Come round if you need somewhere to get away to."

Did she mean drop in for a visit? Or was it an invitation to something more?

He sets off for Bilan's house.

Arn

"I'll get it," he says, jumping up at the sound of the doorbell. He guesses it's Grant. Arn is glad he's there to answer the door, like he lives there. He doesn't trust Grant, remembering how he rubbed himself against Bilan in the gym. He pretended he was showing her how to shoot baskets, like Arn hasn't shown her a thousand times. He opens the door and enjoys the look on Grant's face as he tries to hide his disappointment at seeing Arn there.

"I knew you'd show up," says Arn.

He almost laughs as Grant tries to sound casual. "Hope you don't mind."

Arn gives Grant his long, level look, the one he practises. "Depends what you're here for."

Arn leads the way in. Grant gawks around as he follows. It's like he's surprised Bilan lives in a regular home, with chairs and a TV and books and family photos on the wall. It's like he expected no furniture, and mats on the floor.

Bilan asks, "Did you get a lecture from your father at home?"

Arn closes his eyes as Grant relates everything his father said to him and how he stood up to him. Bilan murmurs, "Well done," and "Good for you," every now and then. After an hour Mrs. Mahamoud calls Bilan from the room. When she returns she says, "Mother regrets that I am not allowed to entertain two boys at the same time, especially when she has no acquaintance with one of them."

Arn says quickly, "Thanks for stopping by, Grant. I'll see you out."

At the door, out of Bilan's hearing, he adds, "If you think she'd go with a preppie daddy's boy jerk-off like you, you've got another think coming. No chance, dickhead."

Despite what he says, he's glad Grant leaves before him.

The next morning Arn arrives at the edge of The Meadows at the same time as Grant.

It's Tuesday, nearly eight-thirty. Another grey and windy morning, with a sky of scudding clouds. The branches of trees in the park are flailing, a few leaves falling and scattering.

Grant says, looking around, "Where's Bilan?"

"Why?"

"No reason. Just you're always together. Seems strange to see you apart."

"That's what you want, isn't it?"

"What?"

"To see us apart."

"Don't know what you mean."

"Liar." Arn moves close to Grant. Taps him on the chest. "Keep clear of her. Don't get any ideas."

Arn hears footsteps behind him and knows it's her. She has this habit, when they're somewhere hidden and no one can see, of trying to sneak up behind him. She tries to surprise him by flinging her arms around him and straddling him with her legs, riding piggy-back. He braces himself, but idiot Grant flinches at the sound of footsteps and whirls around. Bilan, about to launch herself, instead stumbles into Arn.

He says, "Jeez, Grant. What's up with you?"

Grant mutters, "Sorry. Thought you were police, Bilan. They're coming for us today. Dad warned me. I was so wound up after he sounded off at me I forgot to tell you last night."

"You mean you forgot because you were so intent on being a drama queen," Arn scoffs.

Bilan says, "We knew they would take some kind of action."

She links arms with the boys and they saunter across The Meadows. Arn watches Bilan and Grant from the corner of his eye. Was she walking closer to him than to Arn? Was Grant brushing accidentally-on-purpose against her?

Lettie opens the door for them. Barlow is with her. Arn wonders how long he's been there. Like — all night? He looks from one to the other, looking for a sign of something between them, a glance, a touch, a brushing of hands.

Barlow bows as Bilan enters and says, "Good morning, Madam Spokesperson. What's on the agenda today?"

"Same as yesterday."

"Until the police come," says Grant.

Chapter 14

Police Raid

Barlow

Halfway through the morning, on his way back
from the washroom, Barlow sees movement
on the other side of The Meadows. Police are
scattered among the trees. He counts six, one
of them Sgt. Hansen. He's easy to recognize.
He's six and a half feet tall and built like a pole.
His round, rosy face and mop of ginger hair
sticking up all over the place make him look
like he should be in school instead of in charge

of the Savage Harbour police. But he's been in the job for as long as Barlow can remember so he must be a lot older than he looks.

Barlow calls down to the classroom, "Hey, kids. Get this."

The others join him in the hallway. They watch the police move through the trees until they're as near the school as they can get without breaking cover. At a signal from Sgt. Hansen they charge. Barlow hides among the lockers. The others do the same. Peeking out, he sees Sgt. Hansen arrive at the door. He grabs the handle and tries to open it. But Lettie locked it after they had all arrived. Sgt. Hansen puts his face to the glass, peering in. The other police stand behind him, looking around. He points to each side of the door and they set off around the building.

"W-will they see the b-broken latch on the window?" Lettie whispers.

"No way," says Barlow. "Not unless they get real close to it."

Sgt. Hansen paces before the door. He peers in again. Looks all around. Looks at his watch. The other police return, shaking their heads. Barlow is trying to stifle his laughter. Lettie and Bilan, hearing him, start to giggle.

"Better put them out of their misery, eh?" says Barlow.

He strolls to the door while the others go back to class. He enjoys watching Sgt. Hansen's face when he sees him. Barlow waves through the glass.

Sgt. Hansen calls, "Open the door."

Barlow cups his ear, pretending not to hear.

Sgt. Hansen shouts, "Open the goddamn door, Barlow."

Barlow opens the door and makes a sweeping gesture with his arm, inviting the police in. "Good morning, gentlemen. Welcome to St. Isaac's. How can I help you?"

"You can stop playing the fool and tell me what's going on. We got a call from the superintendent saying there was a break-in in progress at the school. I might have known you'd be involved."

"I didn't break in," says Barlow.

"So how'd you get in?"

"Just opened the door. The superintendent was here yesterday. He must have left it unlocked when he left. 'Course we locked it behind us when we came in. You know how important safety and security are."

"We?"

"Just me and a few friends."

"What are you doing here?"

"Studying, of course. It's what you come to school for, you know."

"Don't get smart, Barlow. The only studying you do is of places you think you can break in to. Is your brother here?"

"Haven't seen him since early this morning. I think he was going over to the church to help arrange flowers for next Sunday."

Sgt. Hansen laughs and cuffs Barlow lightly on the shoulder.

Barlow calls, "Hey, police brutality." He staggers sideways clutching his arm.

Still laughing, Sgt. Hansen says, "Seriously now — what are you up to?"

"Told you — studying."

He leads the police to the classroom where the others are working. Only Bilan looks up.

Sgt. Hansen mutters, "Well I'll be . . . You guys really are studying."

"Like I keep telling you," says Barlow.

"But aren't you supposed to be at Laneyville Central?"

Bilan

Bilan stands. "We do not agree with the Education Council closing St. Isaac's and bussing us to Laneyville. And they never asked us how we felt about it. We just want the right to be heard. This is our way of protesting."

Sgt. Hansen grins. "Good for you."

He tells his men, "You guys carry on with regular duties. I don't think these characters pose too much danger to the public." He nods at Barlow as he adds, "Except this one, but I can handle him."

Barlow sits at a desk as Sgt. Hansen wanders around the classroom like a teacher checking on students' work. He asks Arn quietly, "How's your dad doing?"

"Okay," Arn grunts. "No thanks to you."

"Seen him lately?"

"Last month. Once a month."

"Tell him I said hi. How about your mom and the kids. They okay?"

"I guess."

"That's good. Remember I can arrange help if you want it."

"We don't."

"Okay. Just saying."

He moves on to Lettie and says, "How're you doing, dear? Keeping yourself safe?"

She nods.

"Good girl."

He strolls to the front of the room and announces, "I'm sorry to interrupt your studies, folks. I had a call about a break-in in progress at St. Isaac's and I had to check it out. But I'm satisfied no such break-in is taking place. I'll inform Mr. Kitchener, the complainant, accordingly. I'll have to tell him you're here. But as far as I'm concerned you're not causing any trouble and it's not a police matter."

Barlow mutters, "Thanks."

Sgt. Hansen adds, "But you should know that technically you are guilty of trespassing on school property . . ."

Bilan, still standing, interrupts, "Excuse me, but the law states that any person can go onto any property during daylight hours if permission to do so is implied. It certainly is in the case of a school. Especially when it refers to students attending that school who not only have implied permission to enter but are in fact obliged to do so — every day."

Sgt. Hansen and the students stare at Bilan.

Sgt. Hansen says, "You're right. But remember that permission can be revoked."

"Yes — but only by the owner of the property. In this case that is the province. To my belief no such permission has been revoked."

"Mr. Kitchener can act on behalf of the province."

"Has he done so? Has he stated that we are denied entry to our school?"

Sgt. Hansen shakes his head. "Just said there was a break-in."

"In that case we will stay."

Sgt. Hansen smiles. "Sure. Like I said, it's not a police matter. But just for the record — not to share with anyone, including the school authorities — I'll take your names. I know these two gentlemen . . ." He nods at Barlow and Arn. "And I know Lettie, and you're Grant Mograno — right? And . . ." He looks at Bilan. "Ms. Mahamoud, if I remember correctly."

Bilan spells out her name and adds, "I am spokesperson for the Gang of Five."

"That what you call yourselves?"

She nods.

"Cool. So I should call you if I get another complaint or anything like that." As he scribbles in a notebook, Sgt. Hansen tells Bilan, "I'm on your side, you know."

She smiles. "Thank you."

Barlow announces, "Time for noon break. Let's head to the gym." He catches Grant's eye as he adds, "For some good, clean fun."

Sgt. Hansen follows them. He watches for a few minutes as they shoot baskets, then says, "Three on three. Lettie and Barlow and me against Arn and Grant and Bilan."

They play for a half hour before Sgt. Hansen, breathing heavily, says, "I better get back on duty. Thanks for the game, guys." He starts for the gym door, but stops and looks back at the Gang of Five. "Good luck with your protest."

Chapter 15

Bilan's Ambition

The shrill ring of the phone crashes into Bilan's semi-conscious state. It's a siren from an ambulance trying to force its way across Tahrir Square. She's cowering behind her parents in the middle of a crowd. Thousands are shouting slogans as a wall of soldiers advances on them. She should be at school — would rather be at school. But there is none, with the city in uproar and chaos as day follows day of protests, often violent.

The siren stops. Is the ambulance trying to make its way to pick up more injured demonstrators? Or is it already loaded with the injured and trying to get back through the crowds to the overflowing hospital? There the wounded lie on the floor and in the hallways and on the ground outside waiting for treatment. The siren starts again. She opens her eyes. Not a siren. Her phone, on the table beside her bed.

It's seven o'clock on Wednesday morning.

She picks up the phone and Sgt. Hansen says, "Ms. Mahamoud. Bilan. I'm sorry to call so early. But I wanted to catch you before you left for school. Mr. Kitchener has arranged for a security company to guard St. Isaac's, to keep you out. He told me because he wants a police presence there to, as he puts it, 'assist in the arrest of the delinquents that the police failed to apprehend yesterday.' I promised nothing. But I'll have the guys keep an eye on the school from a discreet distance, not to help the security company, but for your safety."

"Thank you, but we will be safe."

"I hope so. I have to warn you, I know this company and its employees. I know the way they work. They are not like the security guards you see at the mall. They're heavy duty and don't mind using force. In fact, I suspect they enjoy it. I don't want to see you or your friends hurt. My advice is to stay away from the school today."

"We cannot do that. It would be giving in to Mr. Kitchener. That would compound the wrong already done to us by the closure of the school."

"I was afraid you'd say that. So I'm ordering you to stay away . . ."

She cuts him off with, "Thank you, Sgt. Hansen."

And she ends the call.

Two hours later, she and Lettie stand on the beach behind the school. After Sgt. Hansen's warning she called Arn and told him to meet on the beach. She asked him to tell

Barlow and Grant to do the same. Then she walked there, taking Shore Road to avoid the park. After making sure there were no guards at the back of the school, she climbed over the wall and broke in. She told Lettie about Sgt. Hansen's call. Keeping well back from the front doors, they peered cautiously out. They saw three guards in front and one on each side of the school. With no guards at the rear, Bilan and Lettie left by the usual window and climbed back over the sea wall.

Grant arrives first. "I'd already left home when Arn called. I'm supposed to be grounded. Grounded — and I'm practically an adult! Supposed to go from the house to the bus stop, get the bus to Laneyville Central, then get the bus home and stay in. Dad even said he'd drive me to and from the bus to make sure I didn't go anywhere else. Who does he think he is? I mean — what century is he living in? So I got up early and snuck out. Who knows what he'll say or do when I get home tonight."

He paces as he talks. Bilan thinks, despite his brave talk, he's on the verge of crying. She takes both his hands to keep him still as she says, "You are fighting oppression on two fronts. Your father who thinks he can dictate what you do, and the council who think they can subdue the student population. You have to stay firm in your opposition to both."

She stares into his eyes, willing him strength. He stares back, and moves closer. She doesn't know whether to pull back or stay still. She knows what he wants, the same as Arn. But she realizes Grant's want is only physical. Arn, having learned his limits with her, is devoted, nevertheless. If she gave in to Grant's advances, she suspects he'd lose interest once he learned those limits. And she enjoys Arn's devotion, at the same time as she finds it almost pathetic. She finds his jealousy stifling. He's jealous not only of any boy who so much as smiles at her, like Barlow, but also of her ambition. She knows he feels it will take her beyond his little world in this little town. She hopes it will.

She glimpses movement from the corner of her eye. At the same time Lettie murmurs, "Arn . . ."

He's sauntering towards them, hands in pockets. Bilan releases Grant's hands and steps back. Did Arn see? She tells herself it means nothing, really, her holding Grant's hands. She's just helping him cope with the situation at home. But would Arn understand? She runs to meet him, and throws her arms around him. He stops, but keeps his hands in his pockets. She can feel his muscles tense as she hugs him. She leans back to look at him but his eyes are on Grant as he asks her, "Everything okay?"

"Grant is in a fight with his dad over the protest."

Arn grunts. "My dad doesn't even know about it. And Mom's too busy to care."

Bilan slips her arms from around him. She takes his hand and tugs him forward so they stand with the others.

Arn is glaring at Grant.

Grant mutters, "What?"

Arn says, "You effin' know what."

Lettie's eyes flicker between Arn and Grant.

Bilan mutters, "Boys . . ."

Barlow arrives, surveys the group, and asks, "So what's going on?"

"Mr. Kitchener has sent security guards to keep us out," says Bilan.

"So we may as well spend the day on the beach, eh?" Barlow suggests.

Bilan shakes her head firmly. "Like I said before, we must give the council no excuse for accusing us of doing anything wrong. Goofing off from school would be wrong. We spend today exactly like yesterday. Only difference is we use Lettie's way in and out of the school. We want the guards to not even know we are here. So we have to keep clear of the front door and all the windows. We will work upstairs in the library, and at the end of the day we leave the same way we went in."

"Laughing all the way at the security guards," says Arn.

Chapter 16

No Resistance

Lettie wakes on the floor beside Barlow.

He stayed when the others left at three the day before. She was nervous about slipping in and out of the school with the security guards still there. She thought they might stay all night. What if they stormed into the school while she was sleeping and dragged her out? Barlow said he'd stay and they could get dragged out together. He had to work at the inn, so she went with him and hung around in the kitchen. They had leftovers for supper and were back at the school by eight. The guards were gone, but he said, "Want me to stay? I can if you like, if you're still afraid."

What did he mean by 'stay'? Just sleep at the school, in the staff room beside her? Or sleep, like, with her, like they were boyfriend and girlfriend? Was it enough to make them an item that they had coffee together at Harbour Java the week before? That they stopped there again last night on the way back to the school when he finished work? That they had supper together last night, even if it was only leftovers?

As if reading her thoughts he grinned. "That's not a proposition. I mean just stay."

Of course. She was silly to think he meant anything else. "P-please." She hoped he didn't hear the regret in her voice.

She sneaks a glance at him.

He's awake and smiling. "Sleep all right?"

She nods.

He stands and stretches. "Let's get some breakfast," he says.

He picks up his jacket and something black and sleek falls out. He retrieves it quickly and puts it in an inside pocket.

She frowns. "What . . . What's that?"

"What?"

"What . . . What you just p-put in your pocket."

He shrugs. Too casual. "Just a knife. I always carry one. You never know when you're going to need to peel an orange, or . . . or sharpen a pencil. Come on. Better go over the sea wall, in case the guards are back."

They walk along the beach until they can peer over the wall and see down the side of the school. Three guards stand at the front corner. They look like aliens, bulky and menacing in their black uniforms, with caps pulled so low over their eyes they seem faceless. She'd been on edge all through the day before, expecting them to barge into the school any time, Mr.

Kitchener at their head. But the Gang of Five studied without being bothered.

She mutters, "Suppose they come into the school and arrest us."

"My advice — go limp," says Barlow. "Make like a rag doll."

"Just . . . just . . . give up?"

"If you're feeling feisty, scratch their face, or go for their eyes. Or kick 'em down here." He points between his legs.

She can't imagine doing anything like that. But neither can she imagine just giving in.

It's eight o'clock by the time they get back to the beach. The wind is blowing in from the sea. It streams low clouds across the grey sky and swirls sand in their faces. Bilan and Grant and Arn are already there. Bilan and Grant are standing close. Bilan has her hand on his arm. Arn is standing apart, arms folded, staring out to sea.

"Grant says he cannot do this any longer," Bilan explains. "He wants to give up and go to Laneyville Central."

"My folks were up early, before I could get out of the house," says Grant. "Dad wanted to know where I was going. I wouldn't tell him. But he guessed I was joining up with you guys and that we were getting in the school somehow. He was still shouting at me as I walked out on him and Mom was crying." His eyes flicker over the group one by one. "I have to go back. Sorry."

He tries to move away, but Bilan holds his arm. "You may as well stay. The occupation is going to be over today if your father knows we are in the school. What does one more day matter when you are in trouble already?"

"So that's it?" says Barlow. "End of protest today?"

"We should jam the doors and barricade ourselves in," says Arn, still staring out to sea.

"They would find a way in, or wait us out," says Bilan.

"So we just give up," Arn scoffs.

Bilan releases Grant's arm and moves

beside Arn. "We accept what comes."

Arn turns his back on her. Lettie wonders if he disagrees with Bilan. Or if he's jealous that she stood so close to Grant and held on to his arm.

Bilan talks to Arn's back. "The point is to make a statement. We have done that. The guards cannot arrest us. They do not have the power. All they can do is evict us from the school. And as soon as we resist, in any way, we put ourselves in the wrong. That undermines our case. Let us go in, like we planned, and see what happens."

Lettie thinks of Barlow's knife. Of his reputation. No one at school ever messed with him. She imagines him resisting the guards. She fears he'll get in serious trouble because of the knife. She fears even more that he'll be hurt.

She catches his eye and whispers, "N-no resistance."

He smiles and winks.

Bilan strides away from Arn and peers over the wall. She looks right and left, and climbs over. Grant hesitates, then follows. Arn doesn't move.

Barlow goes to him. "Don't sweat it, buddy. All she wants is to keep Grant with us today, so the Gang of Five doesn't get broken up. Means piss all. Looks like it's all gonna be over today anyway. And then daddy's boy will be out of the picture."

Arn's face slowly relaxes and his shoulders drop as he mutters, "I suppose." He sets off after Bilan and Grant. Then he stops and scoffs, "So we end the action with hardly a whimper. How pathetic can you get?"

"It's what the boss wants," says Barlow.

Arn walks on.

Barlow calls, "Hey."

Arn stops. "What?"

"But just in case — remember they have pepper spray and batons. Which means get in first."

Lettie's stomach heaves, but she says nothing. She just follows the boys over the wall, and holds Barlow's hand as he helps her down.

They work upstairs in the library for an hour in tense silence.

Then comes the click of a key turning in the lock of the front doors and the scrape as they're pushed open.

Lettie looks at Barlow, sitting beside her.

He mutters, "Remember what I said about scratching their faces and going for their eyes?"

She nods.

"Well forget it. Just go limp, like I said first. Like Bilan said — no resistance."

"You . . . You do the same."

He doesn't answer.

Bilan says, "Pretend you are working, and they are interrupting our studies."

Tramp of heavy feet through the hallways downstairs. Shouts of "No one here."

Silence.

Lettie thinks, wishes, *maybe they'll just go away, leave us alone.*

Then feet clattering on the stairs. Five security guards barge through the open door and stand along the front of the room. Their leader says, "We're here on behalf of Mr. Kitchener to secure and safeguard the premises."

Bilan says, "Thank you, but they are secure and safe already."

Mr. Kitchener and Mr. Mograno follow and stand by the door.

Mr. Mograno beckons Grant. "Come on, boy. Time to be sensible before you get yourself in even more trouble."

Grant looks around at the rest of the Gang of Five. He doesn't move.

Mr. Mograno says, "Now! Last chance."

Grant stands. He looks around again and his eyes settle on Bilan. He mutters, "Sorry," and joins his father at the door.

Mr. Kitchener glares at the remaining

students. "The rest of you — leave the school immediately. Wait for me outside."

No one moves.

Bilan says, "We are doing nothing wrong. We are just studying."

Mr. Kitchener tells the security guards, "Take them out." He points at Bilan and adds, "Her first."

Chapter 17

Riot School

Looking back afterwards, Lettie will think of everything that happens next as taking place over several minutes. But she knows it all happens within a few seconds.

One of the guards strides to Bilan and grabs her arm while she's still sitting at her desk. She says, "All right. I will come," but he ignores her and hauls her to her feet. He starts for the door, still holding her arm and dragging her behind him. She crashes into desks and chairs as she stumbles after him. She trips and topples forward, her hijab sliding from her head. He stops and puts his free hand up to steady her. It lands on her breast. She gasps. He grins.

Arn is out of his seat. He snarls, "Let her go." He runs at Bilan's captor, weaving through desks and jumping over a chair.

Two guards grab him and twist his arms behind his back, surprising him with how easily they overpower him. Every time he struggles against their grip they lift his arms higher, forcing him to lean over.

One of the guards says, "Calm down and you won't get hurt, *boy*."

Bilan is looking back at Arn as she's dragged towards the door, and he's filled with shame that he can't defend her.

Barlow rose from his desk at the same time as Arn, but calmly and slowly. He strolls to where the guards are holding Arn. He smiles at them and says, "Hi, guys. How ya doing today?

We don't want any trouble, you know." As he talks he offers his hand to one of Arn's guards to shake. With a glance at his partner the guard takes his hand from Arn's arm and extends it towards Barlow, who's still talking. "My friend here is a bit hot-headed sometimes, but he doesn't mean anything by it. If you just let him go I'll make sure he stays peaceful now that you've made your point . . ."

Still smiling and talking, Barlow takes the fingers of the guard's offered hand and twists them. Suddenly the guard is howling as Barlow spins him around. The guard releases Arn and flails backwards at Barlow, who twists the guard's hand further, forcing him to bend forwards, like he had made Arn. Barlow leans back and raises his foot. As he releases the guard's hand he boots him hard at the base of his spine, sending him hurtling face first into a desk, knocking it over. The guard's cap flies off and he sprawls on the floor, groaning. He lifts his head and looks back at Barlow, who steps forward and kicks him in the face, snapping his head back against the floor.

Lettie, blinking, fingers flying, can't believe how easily Barlow dealt with the guard. Suddenly he's no longer the easygoing, undemanding companion of the last two days. She feels him moving away from her. She feels sorry for the guard and afraid of Barlow.

Arn's remaining guard lifts Arn's arm even higher as Barlow floors his partner. Arn is bent nearly double, pain shooting up his arm into his shoulder and through his whole body. He forces himself to relax, takes three long deep breaths, then collapses towards the floor as if he's blacked out. He spins as he falls. When he feels the guard's grip loosen, he slips his hand from it and lands on his back. The guard lifts his foot and goes to place it on Arn's chest. But before he can bring it forward Arn kicks upwards, catching the guard between the legs. The guard gasps and doubles over, reaching towards Arn with one hand while clutching himself with the other. Arn scrambles up. He grabs the guard's head and wrenches it downwards as he brings his knee up, slamming the guard's head against it. The guard lies between the desks with one hand holding his nose, which is spurting blood, still clutching himself with the other.

The two guards left at the front of the room have hurled themselves at Barlow. Dean's voice is in Barlow's head. *Go for the eyes and the throat and the nose and the balls. Don't lose your cool. As soon as you do, you stop thinking. Stay on your feet whatever you do. Never, ever go down.*

As the guards rush him, Barlow's hand shoots out. One of the guards reels back, gagging and holding his throat. The other stops and pulls his baton from its holster. Barlow, his eyes fixed on the guard, reaches inside his jacket. Lettie, still watching, transfixed, remembers the knife he slipped in an inside pocket that morning. She recalls the flippant comment he made about never knowing when you might have to peel an orange or sharpen a pencil. She didn't believe him then, and certainly doesn't believe him now. He's moving even farther away from her. She knows if he uses the knife, even if he's defending himself and his friends, it will elevate the encounter into something far more serious than a clash between students and guards. He'll be completely lost to her. She pictures him being arrested by Sgt. Hansen.

The guard with his baton drawn has his back to her. She launches herself from her desk and flings herself at him. She throws her arms around his neck. She glimpses Barlow's eyes and mouth open wide in surprise. His hands — with no knife! — reach towards her as if to catch her. She remembers the feel of them on her hips and waist. Barlow jumps back as the guard whirls around and Lettie is whirled around with him, clinging to him, her feet hardly touching the floor and banging against desks.

Chapter 18

Fighting Back

Grant, standing beside his father, is frozen in shock by the sudden violence, and by his horror at the way the guard grinned when he touched Bilan, and by the way he was dragging her towards the door. Towards him.

Bilan grabs hold of a desk. She plants her feet and leans back, resisting the guard's pull. The guard tugs her. She holds on. Still grasping her with one hand, the guard steps towards her and slaps her. Her free hand flies from the desk to her face. She feels the heat rising from where his open palm landed and imagines a welt there in the pattern of his hand. Tears well into her eyes. She doesn't know whether they're from the pain of his assault or the shame of being slapped in front of her friends like a naughty child.

Settling in Canada, Bilan believed that the way to resolve conflict was through peaceful protest, not with the violence she had witnessed as a child. Now she has a bitter, fleeting revelation: This humiliation and pain is all that belief has brought her. She's had enough of peaceful protest.

She lashes out at the guard with her foot. He grabs it and grins at her as she hops helplessly in front of him. His hand slides from her foot up her leg. She feels it through the thin fabric of her leggings as if there's nothing between her bare skin and his hand. The guard slides his hand behind her knee so her leg hangs over his hand. His hand slides farther, to the back of her thigh. She gasps. He lets go of her leg and turns to see Grant looking at him.

And grins.

Grant hasn't been able to decide where he belongs in the battle. When he went to his father, docile and obedient, he felt he was no longer with his friends. He was part of the establishment, on the side of the school administration. He wavered when Mr. Kitchener ordered the guards to take his friends out. His feelings moved further away from the adults as he watched the guard grab Bilan and start to drag her across the floor. And further still when the guard drew his baton on Barlow, provoking Lettie's brave, hopeless attempt to defend him. The slap on Bilan, and knowing how violated she'd feel by the guard's hand on her leg, drew him even further from siding with the adults. Now the guard turning towards him, grinning, as if man to man. That's the final factor that places him back with his friends.

Grant steps towards the guard.

He balls his fists.

He sways back, weight on his heels.

He draws his right arm back and low.

He holds his left arm poised under his chin, ready to follow up.

He swings his right arm forward as he brings his weight forward. All his weight is behind his fist.

He's long realized he's not the star basketball and rugby player St. Isaac's has made him out to be. But he's been faithfully training for years and is stronger and fitter than he'll ever be again in his life. His right fist smashes upwards into the guard's mouth, splitting the lips and mashing them against the teeth. His left fist follows a fraction of a second later, landing on the guard's nose with a liquid smack. The guard releases Bilan. He puts his hands to his face, trying to staunch the blood spurting from his nose and dripping from his shredded lips.

Arn, seeing Grant's punch from the corner of his eye, flames with jealousy. He, not Grant, should be the one to rescue Bilan from the guard. He sees Grant as moving in on her again. Driven by jealous rage, Arn suddenly moves his hands from where he's holding the guard he's wrestling with to around his neck. He squeezes with the fury of his frustration. The guard scrambles to loosen Arn's grip. His eyes are wide and gurgling sounds are coming from his throat.

Bilan sinks into a chair, one hand still covering where the guard slapped her, the other wiping her eyes. She tells herself the tears are not of pain and fear, but of anger. Anger at the established order and the guards who protect it. She pulls her hijab back in place so that it covers her hair. She wishes it would cover her face.

Meanwhile, Lettie feels as if she's on the tilt-a-whirl at the carnival as she's whirled helplessly around. She is spun once, twice, still hanging on, a third time starting. A series of scenes have passed in front of her. Arn and his guard hold one another's arms and circle like they're dancing. Mr. Kitchener stands with his mouth hanging open as if he's about to say something as he frowns at the violence he launched and that he's responsible for. Bilan's guard marches her towards the door and Grant punches him. Barlow, recovering from his shock at her leaping to his defence, moves towards her.

The guard growls, "Let go of me you freakin' bitch."

Never before has she been spoken to like that. She feels her glasses slipping from behind her ears and moves her hand to stop them sliding down her nose. The movement is so instinctive that she forgets too late that she has to hang on to the guard. Her glasses fly off and her other hand loses its grip. Suddenly she's flying after her glasses and crashing into a desk. She manages to stay on her feet. But she's dizzy and the pain in her hip from slamming into the desk is making her leg buckle. Then the guard punches her in the eye, with another, "Freakin' bitch."

Lettie can't believe it's happening. She doesn't even feel pain. Not at first. The room is a kind of fuzzy blur without her glasses and with her eye watering. But she can make out Bilan slumped at a desk. She can see Grant sucking the blood from his knuckles where he punched the guard. She can see Arn with his hands around the throat of his guard, and Barlow close by, moving towards her assailant. Then the pain from the punch hits her and the room itself is now a giant roundabout and she's the still centre. She finds herself on the floor, crying.

A second later, the guard lands beside her, moaning and rubbing at his eyes. Barlow is standing over him, leaning low between the desks. He mutters, "Bastard." The knife appears like magic and the blade flies open.

She gasps, "Bar . . . Barlow — no!"

At the same time a voice cuts through the fracas. "All of you put your hands by your sides and stand still."

Chapter 19

Aftermath

Lettie

Through half-closed eyes, Lettie sees Barlow's face close to hers. She feels his hands slide gently under her elbows and pull her to a sitting position. The knife has disappeared.

He says, "Can you stand? Do you want to?"

She says, "I don't know who you are."

He kneels beside her. His arm creeps around her shoulders and she leans against him.

The three guards Barlow dropped pick themselves up. One holds his nose with blood dripping through his fingers, another holds his throat, gagging. Lettie doesn't know what he did to the third, the one that landed beside her. But he's still pawing at his eyes as he slowly hauls himself up by holding on to a desk. Arn takes his hands from his guard's throat and pushes him away. Bilan's attacker, his lower face bloody like raw hamburger meat, glares at Grant.

Sgt. Hansen stands in the doorway.

Mr. Kitchener starts, "Thank goodness you're here. These young people are out of control. I want you to take them out and . . ."

Sgt. Hansen cuts him off. "The security guards are here because you hired them. Would you please take them away and wait for me outside."

Mr. Kitchener looks as if he's going to argue. But after hesitating a few seconds he stomps out.

Sgt. Hansen says, "Mr. Mograno, go with them, please, sir."

Mr. Mograno says, "Come along, Grant."

Grant hesitates. Looks around at his friends. "It's all over, isn't it? What does it matter what I do now?" He follows his father and Mr. Kitchener out.

When the guards have shuffled after them, Sgt. Hansen says, "I'm sorry I wasn't here sooner. I had one of the guys keeping an eye on the school, but had to send him on an emergency call. I came over to take his place and saw the guards had gone. I guessed Mr. Kitchener had told them to move in. Is everyone all right? Anyone seriously hurt?"

Barlow still has his arm around Lettie's shoulders. He catches Sgt. Hansen's eye and inclines his head towards her.

Sgt. Hansen kneels beside her and says, "Let's take a look." He peers at Lettie's face and brushes her hair from her forehead. "You're going to have a black eye, my dear. It'll spoil your pretty face for a few days. But you'll be okay. Just get some ice on it as soon as you can." He looks around at the students. "If you're sure you're okay, I'll leave you for a few minutes. I'm going to talk to Mr. Kitchener and his friends. Then I'll be back." He stops on his way out and adds, "This can't go on, can it? Do you think you can come up with some way of getting yourselves out of this with the honour and dignity you deserve?"

They sit in silence until Barlow says, "You heard the man. What are we going to do?"

He helps Lettie to a chair. She sits with her elbows on a desk and her hands covering her face, sniffling. He stands beside her, his arm still around her, his hand resting on her shoulder and stroking her neck. She knows it's the hand that held a knife a few seconds before, the hand she felt on her waist and her hip yesterday. She has to stop herself from shrinking from his touch, even as she loves him for his ruthless defence of her.

Bilan

Bilan holds herself rigidly upright in her chair. She's trying to control her crying and keep her teeth from chattering. Arn, still angry that it was Grant who got to punish her assailant, stands across the room. He's watching her, but not moving to console her. Barlow catches Arn's eye and motions with his head to go to Bilan. Arn walks slowly across the room and stands beside her, without touching her. She looks up at him.

"Sorry," he mutters.

"What for?"

"I should have got that guard off you. Shouldn't have let him treat you like that."

"There was nothing you could do."

"Still, should have been me that slugged him."

No one speaks.

Then Barlow asks, "So, boss lady, what d'you think? What do we do now?"

"I do not care," says Bilan.

"Yes, you do," he insists. "You got us this far. We'll do whatever you say."

She sighs wearily. "It does not matter what we do. We have lost."

"So let's lose with dignity and honour, like Sgt. Hansen says."

"One more day," Bilan says finally. "Let us make them wait one more day. And then we will end our occupation."

"And no guards. No interference," Barlow adds.

Bilan nods. "It is the best we are going to do."

Barlow says, "Okay, Arn? Lettie?"

Arn mutters, "Whatever."

Lettie lifts her head just long enough to nod.

They wait nearly a half hour for Sgt. Hansen to return. Then they wait another half hour while he takes their proposal to Mr. Kitchener and Mr. Mograno. He returns to announce that they have accepted the proposal.

The students can occupy the school for one more day, with no guards and no interference.

"They aren't happy about it," Sgt. Hansen adds. "Especially Mr. Kitchener. He wanted to press charges against you for assaulting the guards. But I told him you'd have the stronger case when it ended up in court. The judge would be faced with five burly men in uniform, armed with pepper spray and batons, and five nice kids. And as there were no weapons involved . . ." He pauses and looks around. "There were no weapons. Right?" They all shake their heads. He prompts, "Barlow?"

Barlow opens his eyes wide. "Me? 'Course not."

Sgt. Hansen nods. "There were no weapons involved. And the only injuries, apart from poor Lettie's black eye, were a few bruises. So they agreed it was best to let the matter drop."

✳ ✳ ✳

Leaving Lettie and Barlow at the school, Arn and Bilan set off home. As they walk across the park, Arn straggles half a step behind. "You've been making up to him all week."

Bilan stops and puts her hands on her hips. "Who?" Although she knows.

"Friggin' Grant."

"Just how have I been making up to friggin' Grant?"

"You let him get a good feel in the gym . . ."

"I told you that was nothing."

". . . And you hung on to his arm on the beach . . ."

"I was trying to persuade him to stay with the Gang of Five."

"It's like you want to be with him, not me. And it should have been me, not him, to get the guard off you. I would have if those other two guards hadn't grabbed me. And . . ."

She interrupts. "Stop your whining and come with me." She marches into the woods beside the path without looking back. She's sure he'll follow. If he doesn't, too bad. She hears his footsteps after a few seconds.

He catches her up and says, "What?"

She pushes him against the nearest tree. Glancing around to make sure no one can see, she leans into him and murmurs, "All I wanted from Grant was for him to stay with the protest. What I want from you is . . ." She presses herself against him and whispers into his ear, concluding with, "Get it?"

Chapter 20

Betrayed

The next morning the four remaining members of the Gang of Five watch the buses leave for Laneyville Central. Then they stroll through Seaside Park. Barlow and Lettie walk together. He reaches for Lettie's hand, but she has her hands in her pockets. Behind them Bilan takes Arn's hand and rests her head briefly on his shoulder. She thinks she was able to convince him she's not interested in Grant.

"This agreement stinks," Arn grumbles.

"But at least it is our agreement, not theirs," says Bilan.

They stop at the edge of the woods and look across The Meadows at St. Isaac's. They step back among the trees.

"Well look at that," Barlow mutters.

Arn spits, "Lying bastards."

Bilan stares at the five security guards strung out along the front of the school, thinking, *It happens every time. Agreements mean nothing to those with the power. They go along with them one day. And they ignore them the next.*

As they stare at the guards, they see Mr. Kitchener leave the school and stroll across The Meadows towards them. He greets them with, "Now you know who's in charge."

Bilan says, "We are supposed to be able to continue our occupation for one more day. You agreed."

Mr. Kitchener scoffs, "School authorities don't make agreements with the students in their care, no matter what Sgt. Hansen thinks. And students don't have a voice, any more than they have rights." He goes on, "I've warned the principal at Laneyville Central about all of you. I told him you weren't to be trusted. I asked him to keep a special eye on you and to let me know if you cause any kind of trouble, or if you fail to observe the school's code of conduct in any way."

He looks around at the students before adding, "There is one thing you might do to contribute something positive to your school records."

Barlow yawns.

Arn stares at the ground.

Lettie is blinking fast.

Bilan's eyes burn into the superintendent as he goes on, "You can write to me, formally apologizing for your actions. And you can promise to obey the authorities and to follow all school rules in the future."

Barlow bursts out laughing. "Your head's even farther up your arse than I thought."

Arn joins in laughing.

Bilan doesn't take her eyes from Mr. Kitchener as he concludes, "The guards have been instructed to keep you out. If you try to get in I'll have you arrested. That's what should have happened the first time you broke in."

Bilan feels the need for more extreme action that seized her as the guard assaulted her change. It crystallizes into the desire to attack those with power and authority. Anyone with power and authority.

Mr. Kitchener stomps away.

They stand in silence for a few seconds.

Then Barlow says, "What a nutbar."

Arn says, "Now what?"

"Screw Kitchener," says Bilan. "We get in the back way."

Ten minutes later they're in their old classroom.

"Seems wrong, just four of us," says Barlow. "I thought Grant might have second thoughts and show up."

"Just as well for him he didn't," Arn growls.

"Don't be too hard on him," says Barlow. "He came through in the end. Slugged that guard pretty well."

Bilan is silent, wishing they'd all shut up about Grant.

Finally Barlow says, "It's like last day of school. So what are we going to do?"

They go upstairs to the library and take turns reading aloud from favourite books. They find old movies and watch them clustered around a computer. They play basketball, two on two, with Bilan and Arn against Lettie and Barlow.

At noon Bilan says, "We may as well end this. There is no sense in just putting in time." She feels the need to say something to sum up their protest. But all she can come up with is, "At least we carried on our occupation for a week. That's longer than I thought we would manage."

"Did it do any good?" Arn asks.

She shrugs. "We sent the school authorities a message that our voices will be heard. We made them know that we will not be ignored." Suddenly she's not talking to three friends in an empty, doomed school. She imagines she is in a town square addressing hundreds of protesters. "We taught them that if they try to oppress us, we will not take it lying down. And if they do not learn from our protest, then we will teach them a lesson they will not soon forget."

She burns with the desire to step up their action to more extreme protest, to revenge. She adds, "There is one more thing we have to do before we leave."

"What's that?" says Barlow.

"Trash the place," she says.

Chapter 21

Contempt

Arn, Barlow, and Lettie stare at Bilan.

"Say that again," says Arn.

"I said — trash the place," she repeats.

"But the whole point of the occupation was to do something other than wrecking the school," says Arn. "You said it wouldn't do any good. That's why I went along with it. Now you're saying I was right all the time."

"I changed my mind," she says.

"If you're gonna do serious damage, let's at

least get some of the computers out of here," says Barlow. "We'll hide them somewhere out the back. Then tonight I'll get my brother to bring the van . . ."

"No," says Bilan. "That would make us thieves."

"Oh — so vandalism is okay, but stealing isn't."

"Stealing is self-serving," says Bilan. "Vandalism is making a statement."

"I thought our occupation was all about making a statement."

"It was. But now we need something stronger. Something that shows our contempt for the school authorities. Like their contempt for us when they did not care how we felt about the school closing. Like their contempt when they set armed guards on us. Was Kitchener not showing contempt when he ignored the agreement and sent guards to keep us out of the school this morning? Was he not showing contempt when he said our voices still will not be heard? This can be our way of showing our contempt for him, and for all of them. Since they have not learned from the occupation, we need to take our protest a step further. We need to avenge their contempt for us. We need to teach them that while they may have the power of being in a position of so-called authority, we have the power of destruction and revenge."

Lettie's eyes flicker between Barlow, Bilan, and Arn. Her fingertips tap furiously together as she murmurs, "N-no."

Barlow shakes his head. "I'm with Lettie and Arn. I'm not into vandalism. You go ahead if you want. But count me out. I'm outta here. Coming, Let?"

Bilan clutches Lettie's arm. "You do not have to do what he says, just because you think he likes you."

Lettie picks up her old backpack, with her sleeping bag strapped on top. Barlow takes it from her and slings it over his shoulder.

She mutters, "B-bye."

Arn and Bilan stare at one another as Barlow and Lettie climb out through the window. They don't see the two of them disappear over the sea wall.

Bilan says, "She was always weak."

"Now what?" says Arn.

"Let us do it," says Bilan.

"No," says Arn.

The Vandal

I come by night, of course. I sneak along the beach and over the sea wall. I climb through the window at the back of the school, the one with the broken latch that everyone seems to know about. It is a black night, with thick clouds hiding the moon and stars. Two o'clock in the morning is the cops' shift change time. So they're busy with paperwork and getting up to speed with what's going on, not that much ever does go on in Savage Harbour.

I drop to the floor from the window. I flick

on my little penlight, but don't really need it. I know my way around, like everyone who's been at St. Isaac's. I play the light quickly around the classroom. Everything is as it always is. A couple of chairs and a desk lie on their sides, a few desks are out of the straight line teachers always seem obsessed with. Four computers and monitors stand on a long table on the far side of the room. It is tempting to steal them. But simple destruction will leave the authorities mystified. They will seek a cause, and sooner or later come to the conclusion that there is none. It is just an expression of hate and contempt for all those with authority and power.

For a few moments, as I look around, I don't know where to start. Then I pick up a chair and hurl it across the room. It lands with a satisfying crunch on one of the computers. The monitor screen is smashed and the keyboard cracked in half. I smash the keyboard of the neighbouring computer into its monitor. I take the remaining two monitors one at a time up onto a desk and drop them. I snap their keyboards over the side of the table. I tip a couple of desks over and break their legs. But it's too much like hard work so I throw a few more chairs around, making sure they break as they land. I play the flashlight around again. The room looks good. I tip a bookcase over and kick the books into a pile in the centre of the room. That's for later.

Down the hall to the computer lab, I flash my light over the wood-panelled walls. I catch a glimpse of the famous stained glass windows over the front doors. I'm tempted to smash them. But it's too risky with the front of the school looking over the park. I have to admit it is a beautiful building, and it seems a shame to vandalize it. But when you're at war there's always collateral damage.

And this is my personal war.

There are twelve computers, like new, in the lab. Perfect. Here comes an easy $10,000 worth of damage. I plug them all in and fire them up.

I trot down to the storeroom which is supposed to stay locked, but of course never is. I take a bucket and fill it in the washroom. Back at the computer lab — I've always wanted to do this — I stroll along the row of computers pouring water over them, causing a series of sizzling and popping sounds. For good measure I throw them all on the floor, too.

Back in the washroom I plug all the sinks with toilet tissue. Then I open the taps wide so the basins fill and water starts to slop over the floor. In the first cubicle, I take the lid off the flush box and rip out the valve and flapper so they don't shut off. Then I flush the toilet. I do the same in the other three cubicles. Then I get out fast. Sudden inspiration strikes me. How much better to do this in the upstairs washrooms, so the water comes through the ceilings. Ten minutes later, mission accomplished. Already water is running across the washroom floors and into the hallways. I take armloads of books from the library and throw them in the flood.

I head back downstairs, careful not to slip in the stream of water starting to run down the stairs and join the water coming from the downstairs washrooms. I should have done upstairs first so my feet wouldn't get wet. But too late now.

I make a quick tour through the other classrooms, breaking computers and throwing chairs around. Then I slosh back to the first classroom through the flooding hallways. I dig the matches from my pocket and light the pile of books, hoping the fire catches and spreads. But what the fire doesn't get, the water will.

I go out through the window. I collect chunks of masonry from the crumbling sea wall to break the windows along the back of the school. It's risky work because of the slight chance of someone being in the park. I wonder how many I can get away with. It's past three, anyway.

Time to retreat. I glance back from the top of the sea wall before jumping down onto the beach. I see the flickering fire in the classroom glinting off the broken windows. I imagine I can hear the sound of water running through the school.

  Job done.

Chapter 22

A Mystery

ATLANTIC DAILY NEWS

VANDALS STRIKE ST. ISAAC'S SCHOOL

Vandals caused thousands of dollars' worth of damage to Savage Harbour's historic St. Isaac's School some time over the weekend.

The damage was discovered by maintenance staff working overtime on Sunday.

They were clearing out the school in preparation for its being put up for sale.

District Superintendent Stafford Kitchener says district staff are still assessing the damage but estimates it will be at least $30,000. Damage included computers and monitors smashed, windows and furniture broken, and flooding throughout the building. A pile of books was set alight in one classroom. The fire looks like it was extinguished by water before it could spread, singeing only a few chairs and desks.

The school was occupied last week by students protesting its closure and their reassignment to Laneyville Central High. Asked whether he suspected those students, Mr. Kitchener said, "I can't comment because the matter is under police investigation. But you can draw your own conclusions."

Sgt. Hansen, of Savage Harbour

police, confirms that nothing seems to have been stolen from the building. He says there were no reports of any kind of damage done to the school during the occupation, and there were no reports of any disturbance over the weekend.

A spokesperson for the students, sixteen-year-old Bilan Mahamoud, told the *News*, "When we left the school at noon on Friday, the last day of our protest, everything was in order. It was exactly as we found it when we started our occupation.

"We wanted only to continue our studies in the school we had grown to love. We are insulted by Mr. Kitchener's insinuation that we are responsible for the vandalism. A vandal is one who wreaks wanton destruction, and that is the opposite of what we want for St. Isaac's. The people bent on the destruction of the school are the officials who have closed it without once consulting, or even informing, those most affected by it, namely, the students.

"We are not the vandals. We are the wronged. We are the innocent."

Chapter 23

Moving On

Lettie

Lettie sits on a bench in Bridgewater, an hour up the coast from Savage Harbour. She's wondering where to sleep. Nights are getting seriously cold and she needs somewhere indoors. There's a shelter for homeless young people if she's desperate. But she doesn't like going there. The helpers expect her to talk to them. They want her to explain why she's not in school and where her parents are. And they seem slighted when she doesn't respond. Maybe she'll try sleeping in the Bridgewater tourist office. She thinks she saw a way of breaking in when she pretended to look for information a few days ago. If not, she'll break into one of the empty houses she's already found shelter in.

She has two jobs. She works a few hours in a convenience store, and clears tables at a diner. They don't pay much, but enough to get by.

She fled Savage Harbour because she was afraid Social Services were onto her. The occupation was too much in the news — her fault for failing to keep herself invisible. And she couldn't face attending Laneyville Central, with all the newness of kids and teachers and environment, and having to sit on a noisy, crowded bus for half an hour twice a day.

And because of Barlow.

After the rumble with the guards, they went to Harbour Java until he had to report for work. He realized he'd left his sweater at the school. She said she'd go back for it and meet him at the inn when he finished. He said he'd find them something to eat. They stood on Water Street outside the coffee shop. He said he'd always take care of her. He touched her face when he said it. She thought he was going to kiss her. She didn't know how she was supposed to respond. Didn't know whether she was supposed to fall against him or hold back. Wasn't even sure she knew how to kiss. Then he pulled back, and said he'd see her later. He said maybe they'd spend a last night at the school.

But Lettie had already decided to move on that night. Barlow was funny, and kind, and thoughtful. She was grateful and flattered by his concern for her and for his protection when the guards moved in. But the easy, almost casual, violence, and the knife, revealed a side of him she didn't know. That side of him frightened her.

But she wanted his sweater. She thought she could wear it and remember him.

So she went back to the school one last time.

Grant

Grant accepts a cigarette from one of the senior high students he stands with. They're on the sidewalk in front of Englishtown Academy. Smoking is forbidden on school grounds, but out here no one can say anything.

The students were there when he arrived by taxi that morning, feeling like a king as he nodded to the driver. "Pick me up here at four this afternoon." He joined them and introduced himself. When asked why he was transferring for his final year from Savage Harbour, fifteen minutes up the coast, he made a casual reference to "a little trouble at the old school." They knew immediately what he was talking about. They'd heard about the occupation and the vandalism. They pressed him for details and believed everything he said, including his exaggerated account of his role in the rumble with the guards. They nudged each other when he described the way he punched out Bilan's captor, and her gratitude afterwards.

"How did she thank you?" one asked, grinning.

"No comment," said Grant, trying for a discreet smirk.

"What about the vandalism?" another pressed. "Were you involved in that?"

"No comment," said Grant again.

Result: Instant hero status.

He didn't say anything about his real reasons for agreeing to attend the Academy. He wanted to forget his mother's distress at his defiance of his father, her crying and begging him to do as his father wanted. He just accepted his father's offer to increase his allowance so he'd be able to entertain the new friends "of the right sort" he'd make in Englishtown.

After that the daily taxi ride was just the icing on the cake. It was way better than spending half an hour twice a day on a noisy, rickety bus stinking of little kids.

He'd miss Bilan, of course. He feels himself

stirring every time he thinks of how she felt in the gym when she backed into him and started to grind against him. He's sure that if Arn hadn't returned when he did, he could have murmured a meeting place in her ear for later. And she would have been there. But already, watching kids arrive at his new school, he'd picked out a few girls, especially in the lower grades. They were young enough to be flattered by the attention of a senior high student, and might serve to make up for what never happened with Bilan.

One of Grant's new friends flashes half a dozen pastel-coloured capsules at him before returning them quickly to his pocket. "Something better than a smoke for noon break, to ease your way through the afternoon," he says, with a glance around. "That's if you've got the money."

"No problem," says Grant.

He has his new, generous allowance.

Barlow

"So where were you Friday and Saturday night, anyway?" Dean calls after Barlow as he sets off on Monday morning.

"Just hanging out around town," says Barlow.

"But you're in the clear," Dean presses. He's talking about Sgt. Hansen's visit the night before.

Barlow laughs. "Sgt. Hansen says he knows it wasn't me that did the vandalism because I would have taken the stuff, not wrecked it."

"Good," says Dean. "We don't want the police coming round here any more than we can help."

Barlow is off to get the bus to Laneyville Central for the first time. Lauralee, Chelsea, and Sharlane flutter past him on Atlantic Avenue, waving and giggling. Watching them, he thinks of all the girls who fawned over him during his years at St. Isaac's. Although he helped himself to one or two, maybe three or four, he couldn't care less about any of them.

But then there was Lettie. Sgt. Hansen asked about her the night before. He said that not for a moment did he believe she was the culprit, but it was suspicious the way she'd disappeared. Barlow said he didn't know where she was.

Barlow thought he was just being nice to a poor kid, talking a bit to her at school when no one else seemed to, getting food for her from the inn. But all the time it seemed she was doing something to him, kind of hypnotising him, without meaning to. Her effect on him had something to do with her shyness. It was the way she didn't try to impress him or anyone else with how she dressed, or with her conversation — certainly not her conversation. And the fact that she didn't use her looks to try to get her own way. Then when she had him totally hypnotised, when he thought he was looking out for her, she decides she's done with him.

Girls, eh?

He skirts the crowd of kids waiting for the bus. They look at him warily. He stands apart, among the trees at the edge of the park.

Arn

On their way to the bus to Laneyville Central, Arn watches Bilan from the corner of his eye. He's as smitten as ever with her. But he no longer knows quite who she is. She's still smart, and fascinating in her foreignness. And of course she's still heart-stoppingly gorgeous. But she's also an activist and a demonstrator. She sounded like a politician when she started the occupation. And like a revolutionary at the end of it. Then she suddenly urged them to vandalize the school. It frightened him. In the end he left her alone at the school, although he told Sgt. Hansen they left together. He went to see her on Sunday. He said he was sorry for walking out, and told her he lied for her, but she didn't seem impressed.

It proved what he'd already suspected from the moment she started to talk of vandalizing the school. There was only one thing he could do that would impress her.

Bilan has read all the information she can find about Laneyville Central. She's already telling Arn all the rules she's going to challenge. It's no longer controversy, like with the occupation, as protest, but controversy for its own sake.

With her at the centre.

Arn wants to talk her out of her plans. He wants to be the restraining influence she used to be on him. But he knows he'll be beside her in any protest, just as she stayed with him. If he doesn't stay, there'll be plenty of boys — men — who will. And it won't be because they share her beliefs and want to support her, but because they want her. Period.

He reaches for her hand. But she has it tucked behind her briefcase. He lets his own hand fall back to his side.

Bilan

Walking beside Arn, Bilan wonders how long she'll stay with him. She enjoys his pathetic devotion. But he's no longer as interesting as he was when he was full of rage. She no longer wants to try to talk him out of puerile acts of vandalism. Maybe it's time to move on to a new project.

She takes his hand, knowing he wanted to take hers a few seconds before. It's only a minor infraction of Laneyville Central's 'no affectionate touching' rule. But it's a good start to her campaign to challenge the rules of her new school. She hopes someone sees and reports it. She plans to hug Arn openly once they arrive at the school, and to walk in with her arm around him.

There's also the rule about uniforms that violates her right to freedom of speech and expression. She's already breaking that rule by wearing a sweater that is bright red instead of the regulation green. She's wearing her hijab, of course, and hopes the school has a rule against it. She hopes it provokes controversy among students and staff. She's thinking of wearing her full burka. And she'll contact the Civil Liberties Union as soon as anything is said, as she's sure it will.

As she and Arn approach the bus stop, she feels the eyes of all the kids on her. She walks through them as if they don't exist. She has no time for them. They betrayed her with their failure to join her protest.

She nods to Barlow, standing apart among the trees. She'll have to get to know him better. She might need the ruthlessness he showed in the fight with the guards in her future protests.

As the buses approach, the morning sun creeps above the houses. It sets the faces of the excited students aglow.

But Bilan and Arn and Barlow still stand in the shadow of the trees in Seaside Park.